T5-AEX-881

The Derby Man

The Derby Man

GARY McCARTHY

DOUBLEDAY & COMPANY, INC.

GARDEN CITY, NEW YORK

1976

All the characters in this book
are fictitious, and any resemblance
to actual persons, living or dead,
is purely coincidental.

ISBN: 0-385-12408-2
Library of Congress Catalog Card Number: 76-10519

Printed in the United States of America
First Edition

To Paul Eldridge

The Derby Man

Chapter 1

The three men crouched hidden in the trees. "That's him!" the shortest of them whispered. Immediately, his two companions moved deeper into the shadows. "A regular pigeon, ain't he? Comes struttin' through this park every morning at eleven, plump and ready for the pickin'."

The tall, unshaven man beside him growled, "Shut up! We'll jump him when he comes even with us."

But the short excited one wasn't satisfied. Nudging the third man, he persisted, "What do you think, Al? Ain't it just like I told ya–plump, fat and wealthy."

Al moved his big, muscular frame into a better position and scrubbed his perpetually running, caved-in nose on a filthy sleeve. "Yeah, Shorty, ya done good. The bird looks ready to be plucked. Probably has enough money in his wallet to keep us drunk for a month. And he sure as hell ain't going to outrun us like that last guy you spotted."

"Oh, Al. How was I to know . . . ?"

"Shut up!" repeated the tall, thin man. "Here he comes."

A moment later the three muggers leapt out into the path of Darby Buckingham.

"Your wallet, mister, and fast if you don't want a beating first!" Al said menacingly.

Darby stopped, dropping his leather-bound case to the grass. "Gentlemen," he said, his black eyes going from one man to the next and finally resting on Al, "I have nothing of value on my person, and I do wish you would reconsider your demand."

"Listen to him," giggled the man named Shorty. "Did you hear that? He wishes we'd reconsider our demand."

Al drew a deep breath into his broad chest and balled a massive scarred fist into a knot.

"One last time, fat man, that's all I'm going to ask."

Darby sighed. "In that case, I suggest you attempt what you have planned."

The three men began to circle him, moving with practiced precision—Al coming in from the front, hairy arms up, mouth half smiling, the other two pressing in from the sides.

Darby Buckingham launched his squatty five-foot-nine-inch, 255-pound body straight at Al. He took one quick step forward and sent his immaculately manicured fist crashing through Al's rotting front teeth, lifting him into a high, flying arc. The tall, thin man hit him a punishing blow to the side as he swung to grab Shorty by the neck. Clutching the little man as one would a chicken, Darby propelled him up into the air, and, one-handed, sent him smashing down into the thin man, the two pounding to the earth. They had not completely settled when he reached down, grabbed each by the collar and cracked their heads together with an amazingly loud thunk. Several yards away big Al lay staring dazedly toward the thick branches high above. Darby surveyed the three thieves with repugnance. It was over. He picked up his undisturbed case and eyed it distastefully; then he continued on with his short jolting stride.

Disdaining the best efforts of the city's carriage drivers to run him over, he marched down the avenue. At one point he angrily stuffed an expensive-looking cigar into his mouth, lighting it on the move. Three blocks later, he tossed it disgustedly into the gutter and turned in at a huge building.

Darby, still somewhat askew from his recent interruption, looked like a mean, short-tempered bear as he bowled through the outer offices of the New York Publishing House without pausing to look either right or left. At the door of the office marked simply "President," a worried-looking secretary partly rose from behind her desk. She started to speak but, observing the ferocious scowl on the angry face and the bristly way his mustache stood out, she completely lost her nerve and said nothing.

Darby's hand hit the doorknob with such force that it set the kerosene office lamps quivering on the outer room walls. The door exploded inward to reveal a half-dozen carbon-copy, black-coated men wearing looks ranging from outright fear to the shocked indignation borne by the central figure seated behind a massive desk. An expression of concern replaced the initial emotion and furrowed the prominent brow of J. Franklin Warner, President. The plaque on his desk harmonized with the dark burnished paneling of the walls, the heavy gold-woven draperies, and the magnificent Persian carpets that suggested, even to the most casual of observers, that to be president of New York's largest and most successful publishing house was not to be taken lightly.

Ignoring the others, Darby Buckingham strode to the desk like a fat, aggressive beetle and said, "Mr. Warner, here's your latest Western dime novel."

Then, before the eyes of everyone, he gripped the manuscript in both hands and began to pull. Though Darby was slightly past his prime, and considerably overweight, there wasn't a man watching who wasn't captured by the enormous power that caused his straining body to pop vest buttons and split the seams of his heavy woolen coat as if they were paper. The manuscript was several inches thick and the man's stubby round fingers fought to hold purchase. As he pulled, his neck seemed to sink into his body. His massive chest and shoulders heaved upward and swallowed it so entirely that it appeared as if the bacon-slice streak of mustache would rest almost on his collar. So overpowering was the effort that no one spoke and each listened for the tearing sound that must come from either man or book. The paper began to come apart in the grasp; the top pages gave way first and then the book tore itself in half. As it did so it flew in every direction to settle to the floor, the desk, and upon the spectators.

Darby Buckingham smiled and drew his suit back about himself. Slowly, like a giant tortoise, his neck began to emerge as his shoulders settled. The transformation was over in a moment, yet it was so gradual that none could quite imagine how the dynamically powerful man before them had dissolved into the fat, slightly out-of-breath, harmless-looking character they now beheld.

"I'm finished, Mr. Warner. I've written my last gunfight, cattle stampede, and roundup. I'll never again lie and exaggerate and delude my readers. The book that I just dismantled represents the end of my fairy-tale Westerns. In short, Mr. Warner, I quit!" Then, adjusting his black derby, he cheerfully walked out.

It was almost a full minute before anyone spoke. "That's the book we've all been waiting for, Mr. Warner. We've had hundreds of requests from our readers who are anxious for Mr. Buckingham's latest novel."

"That's right," said another. "My circulation department has been stalling off our readers only by telling them that another book would be out in the next few weeks."

"Sit down, gentlemen, sit down!" the president said impatiently. "I am aware of what this means to us; believe me, I am. Darby Buckingham's novels have helped us through lean years and accounted for a good share of this company's profits in the good years. Gentlemen, I don't have to tell you what the reaction of our stock holders will be when they catch wind of this." The solemn faces before him said that he didn't.

"How could Darby do this to us?" asked an assistant editor. "Haven't we always met his every demand?"

"Why, he's the highest paid Western writer in the country today!" another man said bitterly.

"He's greedy; he wants to get rich off us," snapped the assistant editor.

J. Franklin Warner began to drum his fingers pensively on his desk top. The others returned to their seats. "I don't think it's more money he wants. If it were simply a matter of money," he said musingly, "why would he tear his manuscript up?" The question was met by an interesting assortment of ahh's and suitably appropriate exclamations of agreement. When they died out, the president continued, "No, gentlemen, it's not money. I'm afraid it's something that's going to be much more difficult to deal with."

"But what?" someone asked.

"I don't know, but I shall make it my first order of business to find out, I assure you. Whatever is bothering our Mr. Buckingham, it must be taken care of at once. The New York Publishing House will not take this loss!" Then, rising from behind his desk, he smiled and said, "Now, gentlemen, let's set about gathering together Mr. Buckingham's latest book. With a little effort and a lot of glue, we'll have it back together in no time!"

So saying, the management of New York's largest publishing house went right to work.

Chapter 2

At precisely nine o'clock the next morning, J. Franklin Warner stood at the door of 117 Plaza Street, Apartment B. Drawing himself up with a look of resolution, he began to rap authoritatively.

A gasp squeezed its way through the cracks: "Come in, the door's unlocked."

Mr. Warner, surprised by the strangeness of the voice, quickly checked his address book. Then, apparently satisfied, he cautiously opened the door.

Darby Buckingham lay facing upward toward the bottom of an enormous oak desk that he quiveringly held at arm's length. Round, glistening beads of sweat were popping out from his forehead and, without moving his eyes from the crushing weight, he sputtered, "Sit down, sir!"

The man sat and watched as Darby lowered and raised the huge desk five times, then carefully placed it down behind his head, so gently that not even a book or paper shifted.

"My God, Mr. Buckingham! How do you manage to do it?"

Darby smiled. "I don't suppose you knew I was once a professional boxer and circus strong man as was my father before me."

"No, I was quite unaware of the fact," admitted the publisher.

"Well," Darby said, "that was some and many good bottles of ale ago, but I still like to keep in practice lifting. It's clean and simple; it relaxes me and keeps me in appetite." Then, unpuddling his bulk, he rose to face his former employer. "An unexpected pleasure, Mr. Warner. I really must apologize for my rude and abrupt manner in your office yesterday. I became very agitated over that manuscript and I'm afraid I lost my temper and behaved rather badly."

"No, no, not at all. Really, Darby, you put on quite a show. And I know the enormous pressure your writing placed upon you. It's quite understandable that you would speak rashly . . ."

"I did not speak rashly, sir!" Darby bristled. "I meant every word I said."

"But surely you don't mean that. Think of your readers, Mr. Buckingham! Think of the New York Publishing House!"

Seeing the pleading in his former employer's eyes, Darby felt a twitch of remorse and his round face lost a little of its resolution.

The change was not missed by the publisher, who pressed ever more earnestly with his plea. "We have thousands of people who are most interested in your works on the West. You know how well your last book was received."

"It was garbage, Mr. Warner, not a shred of truth in its entirety. All lies! I will not be a part of that sham any longer!"

Darby's black anger was starting to mount and so the publisher tried a different tack. "Look, Mr. Buckingham, it's true that we elaborate and slightly exaggerate the men of the West, but that's what the readers want. They want heroes bigger than life, with guns in both hands, dealing death to bandits or Indians."

As he listened, Darby's head shook negatively. "It is true they want heroes, men who are afraid of nothing and are of principle and courage. I think there are such men to write about without inventing them. Mr. Warner, the West is the last frontier where daring and toughness are what counts. There are men worth writing about besides the legends like Crockett and Hickok."

"But, Mr. Buckingham," the immaculate publisher cried, "with few exceptions, those men out there are lawless. They're barbarians! No one in his right mind would choose to live as they do."

Darby smiled, "Perhaps most of what you say is true. Certainly they have chosen to live without many of the comforts. And, as you say, each man makes his own law, lives by his own code–the true mark of the barbarian. Still"–he hesitated –"I'll wager you there are men of honor and idealism, men almost to match the larger-than-life stories we Easterners fabricate for our readers."

"That's preposterous, Mr. Buckingham! They are just ordinary men; *we* have to portray them as bigger than life."

"I disagree. In my work, I have heard of Westerners who were said to be gentlemen and yet fighters, men who will, in time, tame the West and make it a fit place to raise families."

Upon hearing this, the publisher scoffed: "Perhaps what you say is true, but I doubt it. Name me a man such as you speak of."

"Well," Darby said, "offhand, I can think of none. But I will research the subject and present a list of possibilities within the next few days."

The publisher nodded. "Very well, Mr. Buckingham. I shall eagerly await your list. In the meantime, do you think it possible, in the matter of your latest work, we might . . ."

"Absolutely not! Mr. Warner. The thing is trash; the question is closed."

Although he was not at all willing to see the matter dropped, the publisher wisely chose to suspend the subject for the time being. So, picking up his hat and bidding his most successful Western writer good day, J. Franklin Warner departed. Returning to his plush company office, he felt entirely confident that he would soon be able to return the angry Buckingham to the status of the most widely read Western writer of the time.

Darby Buckingham immediately set about his research. He

read periodicals, books, and news clippings. In his own personal Western library he had access to thousands of bits of information, most of which, he ruefully concluded, were as fictionalized as his past novels.

What he was searching for, he realized, was a man who had never been sensationalized in written form. He wanted a man who hadn't sought publicity or the fame it brought, but rather a person who spoke by his actions more ably than his words.

It was two nights later, when he was beginning to despair, that Darby found the single paragraph in a two-year-old newspaper which read:

> Sheriff Zeb Cather of Running Springs, Wyoming, recently thwarted the fourth bank holdup attempt since he took office eight years ago. Two of the robbers were mortally wounded by the sheriff as they emerged from the Wyoming Federal Loan offices shortly after lunch time. Another man was shot as his horse raced out of town. This man, however, did not possess any money sacks and the sheriff immediately ran him down before he had ridden much distance. All three men had been wanted in several states for bank robbery and murder. This fair town has come to expect this kind of protection from its sheriff, a man whom the locals feel is the best lawman in the territory.

Darby read the paragraph three times and shut his eyes as the holdup scene ran through his mind. Three bank robbers, heavily armed, running out into the street, seeing the sheriff, and going for their guns. Shots, so fast they almost blended; then two men going down with the money in their lifeless, clutching hands. A third leaping to his horse and riding off, foolishly firing back at the sheriff, and taking a bullet for the trouble. His imagination churning now, Darby saw Zeb Cather sprinting for a horse tied at the hitching rail, vaulting into the saddle, and spurring away in chase. So unnerving was Cather's courage and deadly his gun that the remaining robber, in mortal fear, threw his gun away and gave himself up–a move which saved his worthless hide at least for as long as it took the next judge to ride in and set the hanging date.

Darby Buckingham smiled and reached for an expensive Cuban cigar. "Zeb Cather," he uttered aloud, "I like the sound of it!"

With the cigar clamped firmly between his teeth, he continued his research through the night. By dawn, he was satisfied that Zeb Cather was a relatively unknown, unheralded, and legend-sized western lawman. He had come across only two other brief notices on the sheriff of Running Springs. One described a shoot-out where he had outdrawn a noted gunfighter; the other was a small blurb about a range war he had settled several years earlier in Montana.

Piecing the three articles together, Darby tried to picture the face and form of the man and, automatically, his imagination conjured up a tall, lean-hipped, broad-shouldered fighter. In his late thirties, like myself, he thought, but without the stockiness and bulging middle. A Stetson and high-heeled boots, of course, rather than his own derby and round-toed black shoes. Although most of his western heroes wore two six-guns, Darby suspected that this was the exception rather than the rule. Zeb Cather would need only one gun to handle his troubles.

The morning was fully begun when the writer crawled under his desk and hoisted the massive affair up and down for a few minutes, then showered, shaved, and dressed. As he stepped out of the apartment with the three news clippings in hand, he began to whistle. It would be good to show Mr. J. Franklin Warner that there were men in the West big enough to write authentic, exciting Western dime novels about.

The publisher sat at his massive desk and regarded Darby Buckingham skeptically. "Just because you have a few lines of print on this Sheriff Lather . . ."

"Cather, Zeb Cather," Darby interrupted.

"Anyway, it doesn't mean he would be worthy of our . . . oh, your readers' attention. Frankly, Mr. Buckingham, you of all people know that they pay money for action, more action than one man could possibly have experienced."

Darby's wide black mustache began to twitch irritably. "This man has settled a range war, outdrawn a gunfighter, and stopped *four* bank robberies! What else he's done, we don't know. I tell you, Mr. Warner, Sheriff Cather is a man whose story our readers will buy."

"You hope. The truth of the matter is that you're New York Publishing House's top Western writer. The public snaps up everything you churn out. So what if it is a shade glorified? I say you should stick with what is successful. It's what our readers crave; they want to believe the cowboys, gunmen, and sheriffs are as you have depicted them. Really, Mr. Buckingham, why don't you give your loyal readers what they want?"

"Because I can't," he admitted. "My mind and imagination revolt at turning out another page of western fantasy. My readers deserve more than I've given them. I want to go out West and see for myself what it is really like."

For a moment neither man spoke, so shocked were they at the sudden revelation. Finally, the publisher whispered his disbelief. "But Darby, my friend, you are a man of culture, a creature of comfort. You like fine gourmet restaurants, expensive cigars, the opera, books, the theater—all the things that the West is without. Surely you don't really want to leave?"

"No, I guess I don't, Mr. Warner. And what you have said is true. But if you expect me to return to writing, then I must go; my mind has become a sterile wasteland."

Sighing deeply, the publisher studied his hands and realized his defeat. "Where would you go?"

"To Running Springs, Wyoming, to do a book on Sheriff Zeb Cather."

"And how long do you think such a venture would take?"

"Six months, no more, and I'll be back with my best work ever."

"Has it occurred to you, Mr. Buckingham, that you will need a good deal of money in order to sustain your apartment here in New York and to travel? Also, you will want to live in the least offensive manner possible among that riffraff."

Darby smiled. "I believe I have sufficient funds for such an undertaking. As you well know, my royalties have enabled me to amass a considerable . . ."

"It won't be necessary for you to draw upon them, Mr. Buckingham. This firm will pay all your expenses to Wyoming." The president of the New York Publishing House smiled expansively.

Darby grinned in reply. "At what cost to me, Mr. Warner?"

The directness of the question surprised the publisher. "Well," he spluttered, "we would like to publish your latest book, *Singing Six-Guns.*"

Darby scowled darkly, but the publisher pushed bravely on. "It's been six months since your last novel. If your next book on the sheriff of Running Springs isn't out for another six months, your readers will be furious. Really, Mr. Buckingham, we must be fair to them!"

Darby scowled even more deeply. He knew J. Franklin Warner was right; he wasn't being fair. "But I destroyed it, right here in this office," he said hopefully.

The publisher smiled. "No, you did not destroy it; let's just say you temporarily rearranged it." Then, pulling out a block of ragged sheets and waving them over his head: "Here it is, *Singing Six-Guns,* and we're ready to publish if you just say the word!"

"Very well," Darby said, snorting. "I'm leaving tomorrow, and now I must go pack."

"Yes, yes, of course. Your royalties will be forwarded each month, along with cash for your expenses. Take care and return from that wilderness as soon as possible. In the meantime we will keep your office and apartment aired and dusted for your return. Don't get shot."

Darby laughed ironically. "Believe me, Mr. Warner, I only intend to write about the western adventure, not participate in it!"

But later, as he began to walk down the pleasant familiar city avenues, Darby began to believe that, like it or not, he *would* participate in it. Reassuringly, he pulled in his stomach, stretched to the limit of his five-nine frame and, very surreptitiously, flexed and felt his enormous right bicep. Beneath the half inch of soft flesh that wrapped it, a muscle crouched as hard and large as a lamp post. Darby smiled and thought, if pure strength is any attribute for survival, I'll make it . . . even out West.

Chapter 3

Everett Randall's wiry body swayed with the horse as it loped splashing across the mountain creek and charged up the off bank. Dirt and rock cascaded down into the muddied water where the animal's hooves had cupped into the soft creek bed.

"Whoa!" he said. And then, talking to himself as was his custom: "Another five miles and we've got it made. Annie will be surprised we got back so soon–a week earlier than last year's drive."

The man sat, letting his horse blow, and his eyes lifted toward the high Tetons, beginning to tinge red and orange with fall colors. He tried to locate where his cabin would be and traced a finger down from a familiar peak that overshadowed a thickly wooded canyon. Three months driving his small herd to market into Kansas hadn't dimmed the image that he had held over almost a hundred campfires. Everett Randall swore reverently as his eyes stretched down the ragged line of mountains–it was a sight that he'd never grown tired of looking upon.

He reached behind him and unstrapped a saddlebag. Carefully, so as not to smudge the fresh white laciness, he peeled back a brown wrapper and peeked at the material he had bought for Annie. It made him feel good to think of how her face would light up when she saw it. There was enough for a dancing dress to make her look prettier than most girls half her age. Everett snapped the saddlebag in place and pushed on toward the mountains.

Two days earlier, daylight had revealed frost on the ground. Annie Randall looked through the trees and far out onto the prairie. Goodness! she thought, I'll be glad when he gets back! The absence made a woman appreciate a good man even more. With two daughters and a son gone, east and west with marrying, she and her man had grown closer through the years. Everett was past sixty, she knew, too old to be cattle driving. Still, it had been their only choice, because Wyoming cattle prices were rock bottom. They needed money, and at the Kansas railhead market at Dodge City the buyers paid cash.

Looking east, Annie guessed she saw a faint, far-off trickle of smoke. As her gaze traveled upward with the wisping plume, her lips formed a faint line of disdain–the Ratons. They left their mark on this part of the land and, sometimes, she reflected, they even left it on the sky.

Annie moved easily through the morning chores of stock feeding and the cleaning. She liked to keep busy and her lithe form moved with an energy that contradicted her forty-six years.

At midmorning she eased a sloshing wooden bucket of water to the ground and paused for a moment to rest. Her gaze traveled toward the plains in the direction where she guessed Dodge City would lie. Once again, however, her eyes were drawn back to catch the rising smoke of the Raton headquarters. Its presence troubled her today, even more than usual. For she knew of the brothers and their ways. Only four days before, she'd noticed two of them, tall and silent, surveying her from a distance.

Annie picked up the bucket and carried it to her garden. Carefully she poured it down the neat rows. Then, she started to dig at the small beginnings of weeds she never allowed to seed. After an hour she was flushed and perspiring from the bright midday sun, still hot in early September.

Their presence came upon her slowly, like the building of a dark, angry thunderhead over the Tetons. Jeb and Ernie sat relaxed in their saddles and stared at her with brazen, pitiless eyes. Annie swallowed and looked at the ground. She heard their horses approaching. Her hands began to shake and she squeezed them tightly together.

"Howdy, Miz Randall. You sure are a pretty sight on a day like this," Jeb said, eying her length with frank approval. "When's your man coming back?"

Her eyes darted from one to the other, seeking a friendliness she couldn't find. In the younger face, she saw only a laughing cruelty; in the other, there was power that overrode all expression except that of an open love of force. She felt almost dizzy. "Any day now," she whispered thinly. "Any day now, he'll be back."

"Now, Miz Randall, that don't seem possible. He and those other two-bit spreads around here ain't got enough horseflesh nor men to travel more than ten mile a day. I figure ol' Everett is maybe just getting your dinky herd of jackrabbits to Dodge by now. Soonest he could be back would be a couple weeks, I'd guess."

"You . . . you figure wrong, Mr. Raton! Now, if you don't mind, I got work to do," she said, picking up the sharp-pointed stick she preferred for weeding.

They sat waiting and watching as she worked. The sun seemed much hotter now and her back began to ache from the constant bending to the stick. The last remote suggestion of a weed was gone, but she kept poking the ground, turning up, covering, uncovering, and still she knew the Ratons were waiting.

What, she wondered, could they want? And even as she asked herself, she knew, and shook inside. Her mind swirled across the yard to the cabin and pictured the old Colt revolver, loaded, sitting behind some dishes on the counter. She slowly began to dig toward the house, sweating, aching, wanting to move fast but afraid of what would happen if she did.

Annie was at the corner of the garden now, and she stopped to snatch at an imaginary wisp of greenery. As she lifted up, her eyes caught the distance to the house, then tried to gauge it. Thirty yards! not one less–she'd never make it. They'd ride her down first and, with the fear of it, she would have no chance. The gun, her mind went to it, remembering the cracked walnut handle, the worn heaviness of it–there was power to match the men who waited for her.

"Seems to me those weeds are all gone, Annie. You look plumb run out to me–don't she to you, Ernie?"

"Yeah," he said. "I think we ought to take her inside and lay her down to rest, Jeb."

Jeb winked at his brother. "That's a good idea. Seems to me only neighborly," he said as they stepped down from their saddles.

She jerked upright, the pain flashing through her back, and hurled the heavy, pointed stick at the rapid striding Jeb Raton –then, without waiting to see if it scored, she ran. A scream split the yard somewhere behind her and it put new life into legs that no longer ran with the long, graceful speed they'd once possessed.

"Son of a bitch! she almost blinded me!" he screamed. "Git her, Ernie. Git her good!"

She tripped on her skirts and sprawled on the porch. Behind her she could hear the man's cursing and panting. And over it all–the pounding of his heavy boots. Scrambling to her feet, she shoved the door in, slamming it hard into the wall. Annie Randall heard his steps hit the porch as she reached the counter. Throwing dishes shattering to the floor, her fingers found the gun as he came through the door. It came up then, heavy and with even more power than the man possessed, and, facing it, he screamed and went down in the blast and the smoke.

She was staring at the writhing, sobbing man when Jeb Raton burst through the doorway. In a crimson fist he held a gun, and a long furrow of blood and skin plowed raggedly across his face. The next instant there was a roar within the small, clean cabin, and Annie Randall was gone.

"You're gonna live. The bullet only grazed along the top of your head."

"I thought I was going to die!" Ernie gasped. "That woman would have killed me."

"Hell, think I don't know that? She damn near took out my eye," Jeb swore, wiping blood that welled up from the long gash high on his cheek and dripped wetly to the floor.

"Jeb, what do we do with her? Sheriff Cather finds out about this, he'll hunt us down, might even be able to stir up a posse. Folks won't like us killing a woman. They won't like it at all!"

Ernie was right. Something like this might unite the whole town against them. Jeb thought of an angry lynch mob and, for one of the very few times in his life, he experienced the hollow, sick feeling of fear.

"Pa won't like this either," he heard his brother say. "He's got set ways and don't cotton to woman-killin', Jeb. He'll whip us good. He'll get out his bullwhip, like he did with Junior two years back. You remember that, he cut him up so . . ."

"Shut up, Ernie! I remember." Jeb frowned in concentration. "Pa and the others think we're out on the flats, checking fence. They won't know—nobody needs to know!"

"But I . . ."

"We make it look like a fire; we burn the place down, with her in it. There won't be anything left for Cather to accuse us with!"

"Hell-fire, Jeb, we can't burn her up!" Ernie choked, going pale, feeling the bile rising to his mouth.

"She's dead, Ernie! Do you want Cather and a posse to come after us? Do you want the crew to beat us, Pa to skin us in strips with the whip? Do you want to hang, huh? Do you want old Everett to be trailing us? You know he don't miss with a rifle. Damn, he'd ambush us within a week after he got back! I tell you, we're dead unless we burn this cabin and make it look like an accident!"

Everett Randall started up the trail on the last mile through the timber. At a certain opening, he remembered, there was just enough room to make out the front roof beams, if you looked just right, that is.

He didn't see it. "Could have sworn that was the spot," he mumbled, guiding his horse around a fallen log and ducking a branch. He spurred the tired animal into a weary trot, an uneasiness upon him. He was still spurring, body pushed forward in anticipation, when he broke into the clearing.

"God, no!" he cried, punching the horse into a stumbling run. "Annie, no, no!"

It was early the following day when he laid the handle-charred shovel down and stood back to survey the mound. "A stranger might think you let the fire get away from you in the night, Annie, but I know better. You weren't afraid of much, but a fire always worried you. What happened wasn't an accident, you'd never have let it happen. I'll find out, Annie, I won't let whoever done it rest till they are planted in hell! Good-bye–I'll be droppin' in to see you when I can."

He turned away, hollow-eyed, gray, shrunken-cheeked, and looking twenty years older than he had the morning before. Everett Randall shuffled down the hill toward the charred ashes and stone. Near where the front door had been, he turned and slowly bent close to the ground. His bloodshot eyes fixed on the earth and he began to move in an ever widening circle about the rubble.

Much later, he came upon the edge of the garden and stopped. For the first time in over an hour, his eyes lifted to survey the neat, weedless rows. She loved a garden, he thought, feeling his throat go tight again. The bucket lay crushing a plant, and he unconsciously moved to pick it up. His hand stopped midway. It was here, he realized, Annie had first seen danger–she'd never have crushed a plant. He began to study the garden more carefully. It had been recently weeded; there were still oval imprints of where she had knelt to work. Off to the right, just outside the garden, he saw the pointed stick she preferred to a hoe. Everett came to it and lifted it up. Blood, and a dried, rolling strip of skin! "Good for you Annie girl, you got him!" he cried hoarsely over the clearing.

The sun was going low to the earth when Everett tied a small sack of burnt-up memories to his saddle. A half-ruined picture stuck between discolored glass, several pieces of silverware, a small blackened metal jewelry box, and a bristleless bone hairbrush that she had loved.

He mounted his horse and rode almost a mile before he suddenly stopped. Two heavy, torn pine-tree branches lay crumpled several yards from the trail. They were brown among green and stood out from where they lay. He went to them and was not surprised to find that the dried needles popped off, brittle, when he touched them. "Two branches, two men! They must have been used to cover their trail." In anger he snapped the thickest branch viciously across his knee. Once, twice, he brought it down hard. But its fiber held. Whoever the murderers had been, he thought, they were strong. Those branches hadn't been splintered off a tree very easily. Everett knew it would have taken even more muscle than he'd had in his younger days. It would take a man like . . . Ernie Raton!

Swiftly his mind went back over what he'd found, piecing

things together. For almost a quarter of an hour he remained motionless with the limbs in his hands. Everything fit. Ernie had the strength, and it would probably be Jeb who'd been with him. Jeb, he had the ruthless cunning. Junior Raton would have been craftier; he had inherited his pa's brains. If Junior had been in on it, he'd have seen that there would have been nothing within a mile to show men had been there.

Jeb and Ernie–they're the ones, he thought, climbing into the saddle. Though he wore no sidearm, Everett Randall was a crack shot with the Winchester rifle that rested in leather under his leg. It was a fact he had never tried to hide, and it was the thing that had kept the Ratons from running him off the range years ago.

Feeling the smooth walnut stock, he urged his horse forward, off the mountain toward Running Springs. He'd let Sheriff Cather in on his intentions–what the man did then was no matter. He was going to pay a visit to the Ratons. He wanted a look at Jeb and Ernie.

Chapter 4

Zeb Cather scowled as his eyes lifted toward the mountains where the Raton headquarters sprawled.

Beside him, looking drawn and old, Everett Randall sat impatiently. "Come on, Sheriff; these horses have got their wind, time is wastin'."

The lawman curbed his anger. "Everett, I told you how it was back at the office. You can't be sure it was Jeb and Ernie. It may have been some murdering drifters; could have been someone else."

Randall nodded. "Yeah, but I don't think so. Things add up. They're the ones."

"Hunches, suspicions, Ev, that's all you got. If we go in there half-cocked, they'll blow us out of our saddles. It's the wrong time and place. If you weren't so stubborn, maybe I could ride back to your spread and dig around, find something that you missed to give us some evidence. Then I could make an arrest and haul them in for questioning."

"Sheriff, why don't you just ride on back to what's left of my cabin and poke around. You won't find anything more, but you're right. Only thing I'm going to do is get myself killed." He reached down and yanked out the Winchester, levered in a shell, and set the butt on his leg, barrel to the sky. "Still, it's going to save you a heap of trouble later on because I'll take them two murderers with me!"

"Dammit, Everett! You know I can't let you just ride up

there by yourself. Come on," he sighed, "let's get it over with. Just one thing."

"What's that?"

"If there's shootin', let me start it."

"Long as I can try to finish it. Long as I can try."

The big, squatty frame house stood clearly in the distance. The two men were only a half mile away when a wolf-sized dog came streaking out from under the front porch.

"Looks like that critter means business, Sheriff."

"Does look mean, don't it?" Zeb admitted, watching as its frenzied barking brought a swarm of men piling outside.

The dog was still several hundred yards out, teeth bared, running low and hard when Everett snapped a shot in its face. It was impossible to tell how close the bullet was, but, by the reaction of the animal, Zeb figured it must have been a matter of inches. The dog swerved and clawed, trying to reverse itself in midstride. A second shot set it howling, digging like a streak for the house. It went under the porch running full tilt.

Cather grinned. "Never saw you shoot better."

"I never have. Maybe now those Ratons will think twice about opening up on us. Maybe they'll at least wait until I have Jeb and Ernie in position."

The sheriff's stomach muscles went tight, "Come on, Ev. They're all waitin' on us."

Bull Raton spat out the side of his mouth and replaced a frayed, shapeless cigar stub between mule-sized yellow teeth. His big stomach strained at the buttons of his dirty gray woolen long johns and ran over the top of his pants. "What they want?" he snapped.

He received no answer, but he hadn't expected one either. The law always meant trouble, and in Cather it had a good man.

"What the hell do you figure Everett Randall is trying to

do," Junior Raton exclaimed, as he watched the yipping dog disappear under the porch, "get himself killed?"

"Easy, boy," the old man said, spitting again. "Let's hear what the sheriff has to say before we make any moves. Cather never has been able to pin anything on us before–I don't reckon he will now."

"Howdy, Bull," the sheriff called.

"Speak your piece, Cather, then ride. Take your friend with you."

"Got some questions to ask first," Zeb said, his eyes going from one man to the next. In a glance, he counted fourteen men and his eyes came to rest on the raw, mean-looking scab running across the face of Jeb Raton. "Looks like you got peeled real good, Jeb. How'd it happen?"

"None of your damned business!"

The Winchester seemed unnaturally loud as Everett levered a shell and poked the rifle barrel toward Jeb's chest. "Look at Ernie, Sheriff. See that strip of hair missing–bullet grazed, I bet."

"We were stretchin' wire; the top strand broke loose, snapped back and got both Jeb and me!" Ernie growled. "What the hell business is it of yours anyway?"

The Winchester swung toward Ernie, who soundlessly swallowed whatever further words he was going to say.

Everett Randall's voice shook. "You killed my wife, Annie; you and Jeb. Now I'm going to kill you!"

Zeb Cather was a fast man with his hands. There were men in pine boxes to prove it. The men at Raton headquarters only saw a blur as his left hand lashed out to knock Everett's rifle off target. At the same instant, a gun materialized in his right hand. "Don't anybody go for it–or I'll put a bullet in them! Same goes for you, Everett." His voice went flat. "I mean it. Now give me the rifle."

"Ride on out of here," Everett pleaded. "This is between them and me!"

"And the law!" Zeb said, snatching the rifle from his

friend's hands and looking into a face that had gone dead except for the eyes.

"Head on back to Running Springs, Ev. I'll be along in a few minutes."

For a moment, the sheriff thought the old man was going to try to use his hands on him. But as fast as the fight flashed up, it died. Everett gave a ragged sigh of frustration, then quietly turned his played-out horse toward town.

"I'm sorry to hear about his wife," Bull muttered, "but if he comes back here waving that rifle around, we'll kill him. He's too damn good a shot to be handled any other way."

The sheriff looked them over, noticing how Jeb's eyes flicked away as his own came to his face. Ernie just stood, with his tree-trunk legs wide set, a glaring sneer on his face. Junior Raton was different from both his brothers. His eyes locked in on Zeb Cather's like those of a snake. Junior was the shortest of the three tall Raton brothers. That was the reason he'd picked up the nickname. Standing just under six feet, he wore the clothes of a man who liked to look at himself–clothes fit Junior well. His broad shoulders cut in sharply to a small waist, about which was strapped the prettiest ivory-inlaid gun Zeb had ever seen. That was the biggest difference between Junior and his brothers: they were just damn good with guns; Junior was the best anyone had ever seen. Some folks who knew Zeb Cather from way back said that Junior Raton was faster than the sheriff had ever been. It was something Zeb didn't want to find out, so he held the Colt steady in Junior's general direction.

Junior noticed the special attention he received and smiled at the compliment. "You're fast, Sheriff, faster than I imagined a man your age could be," he offered expansively. "And you can use either hand or both when you have to. That ain't easy, I know. I'm glad to see you're still so good; it will make drawing against you more interesting."

"Shut up, Junior," Bull Raton snarled irritably, scratching his stomach. "Like I said, Cather, we're sorry about his woman getting killed, but it ain't right to go around accusing hard-working folks like us."

"You never worked a day in your life, Bull."

The man's eyes narrowed. "We don't kill helpless women, Sheriff. I raised these boys right, to respect women. Except the dance-hall ones," he amended, "but them ain't the same. These boys of mine respect a married woman. Ain't that right, Ernie, Jeb?" he asked, turning around to look at them.

"Sure, Pa, sure," big Ernie whined. "Me and Jeb wouldn't have hurt her! Would we, Jeb?"

Jeb was looking right into his pa's eyes, and what he saw made his jaw tremble and spill out the words, "No, Pa—we didn't do it—we didn't, Pa, honest!"

When Bull turned back to face the sheriff, there was a muscle twitching in the side of his face. His gaze was fixed on the ground. "Get on out of here, Cather, while you still can! You heard my boys; they didn't do it."

The sheriff picked the reins up from around his saddle horn. "I think they did, Bull. So do you. I can see it written all over your face, and theirs. Only thing keeps me from taking those two murderers in is evidence. That will come too, one of these days."

Junior Raton swaggered off the porch. "Put your gun away, Sheriff, and let's see if we can't settle things right now."

"It'll come soon enough, boy. You can wait a little longer to see how fast you really are. Another thing," he said, addressing all the men, "if anything happens to Everett Randall, I'll stir up a vigilante committee and we'll hang every damn one of you that we don't shoot first. Remember that, Bull. If he so much as breaks an arm, you're finished in these parts, evidence or not."

With his gun still trained on the men, he backed his horse slowly out of the yard, covering his retreat. When he was out of pistol range, Zeb turned his horse away from the Raton headquarters. It was then he heard the wailing, "No, Pa, no!"

"Get it, Junior. Get me that goddamn whip!"

Zeb Cather was out of sight, but he moved his horse back through the trees to step down and watch.

Junior Raton had a gun on his own brothers. Zeb shuddered as he realized Jeb and Ernie believed he'd use it because their hands were up, and Bull was dragging a long black bullwhip toward them. The first scream tore out of Ernie long and shrill. Zeb shuddered. Not wanting or needing to see more, he spurred his horse toward Running Springs, an icy smile frozen on his face.

Everett's face was as colorless as an alkali flat when the sheriff caught up with him. Only his eyes seemed alive. "They did it, Sheriff. You saw that slash across Jeb's face, and the bullet that plowed Ernie's scalp. You should have taken them in or let me shoot 'em! I will anyway, now."

"If you do, Ev, I'll have to see that you go to jail. I'm sorry, but I would."

"Zeb, with my Annie gone, I don't much care how things work out. The only thing that matters is to see that those two woman-killers get what's coming to them."

"You will! If you help me get evidence." He scrubbed his eyes wearily. "They'll hang for this. I promise they will! But first we have to prove they're guilty."

"How, goddamn it? I got my proof. How you going to come up with yours?"

Sheriff Cather shook his head in despair. "I don't know," he admitted. "I've been after them for years. Bull is too smart to make a mistake I can nail them with. And in the meantime, they keep rustling cattle, robbing, and driving folks like yourself off the range. The toughest part, Ev, is getting close enough to catch one of them in the act or making a slip of the tongue. I can't get near their place without someone spotting me."

"Them boys like to drink pretty good."

"What has that got to do with it."

"Well," Everett said, "maybe they might talk too much at the Concord Saloon some day."

"Not if I was in there."

"Maybe if I was, they wouldn't notice so much."

The sheriff pulled his horse in. "What are you getting at, Ev?"

"Well, I got a saddlebag full of sale money, and not much else. I think I'm going to see how many drinks it'll buy me. Thirty-eight hundred dollars ought to buy a lot of drinkin' time in the Concord. Maybe enough to hear those two say something that will get them hung."

"It's not worth it."

"The hell it ain't! You got any other ideas about how to get close to them?"

The sheriff of Running Springs, Wyoming, felt old, older than he ever remembered as they rode toward town late that afternoon. Maybe, he thought, the best thing would have been to let Everett Randall ride out alone and face the Ratons. They'd have killed him sure, but he might have gotten Jeb and Ernie first, and Ev would have died a happier man with a bullet in him than he would drunk and alone without Annie.

When they rode into town, Everett reined his horse toward the tie rail in front of the saloon.

"No sense going in there now, Ev. The Ratons won't be in tonight." The sheriff might have said more, but he didn't. One look at Everett told him that the man was going to get drunk regardless of what the Ratons did. It just didn't much matter.

Chapter 5

Darby Buckingham peered out through the window of the rocking Concord stage and surveyed the prairie. Except for an occasional broken-down wagon or the scattered bones of some forgotten animal, there was nothing to interrupt the vastness. Still, it had a beauty to it and, as the stage barreled along mile after mile, there should have been a peacefulness about it too. There would have been if it had not been for the singing stage driver. Lighting a cigar, Darby tried to push the sound out of his mind, but it droned relentlessly past his thoughts and overpowered them. As he was forced to listen to the words, he again considered the growing possibility that the driver was a lunatic. For the thousandth time, he heard the first line of what was apparently the only part of the only song the man knew. "Oh my darlin', oh my darlin', oh my darlin' Clementine, you are lost and gone forever, dreadful sorry Clementine."

It was midmorning and the dampness was gone from the ground. It would be hot again, as it had been for days past. The dust began to sift maliciously through cracks and windows, and Darby felt the first trickle of sweat river its way down between his shoulder blades.

Old Andy Carson whacked the roan, who was laying back as usual; the horse immediately took the slack from its harness as it surged forward. Smiling as if he'd been a big-city truant officer making a pinch, he yelled, "Strawberry, ya lazy devil, I caught you again. Gee haw!" The horse, knowing its name, laid its ears back and ran on.

Carson drove with studied indifference. His tough, beetle-brown hands held the reins and worked independently of his thoughts as the big iron-rimmed wheels churned down the path that had already started to rut.

Every now and then, he'd momentarily interrupt his song to send a big, arching stream of greenish-brown tobacco and prairie-grass juice through his whiskers. When possible, he'd wait long enough to drive past a target before letting it fly. Andy Carson had always been the only driver on this stretch and he'd mapped the trail with his spitting in mind. So it was that the ruts occasionally ran crooked, toward one of his targets. No one had ever asked about the deviations, and Andy probably wouldn't have answered if they had.

The roan was starting to ease up, ever so slightly, in its traces. The move was so deliberate and gradual that no one but an expert would have noticed. But, with each stride, the horse was lessening a few more ounces of pressure. Andy smiled; trapping the roan was his sole source of amusement. He'd let Strawberry go for a half hour or so, until it became ridiculous, with the collar hanging loosely; then he'd snap the roan a good one. He never hit the animal too hard, though, for it was the oldest horse in the team and had been pulling the high, rocking Concords far longer than the others. It made a person tired, Andy reflected, the way age got to things! The roan was sort of like himself, in a way. With years and experience, it had learned to use its brain better than the five younger horses.

The driver let the coach veer slightly to the right and it bore down on a greenish-brown ox skull two hundred yards out. "Pweutt!" he went, as the juice jumped into the air and then dove downward to drench the skull. Looking back, Andy laughed as he saw he had connected. It had been a good shot; he'd judged the breeze just right again. "Oh my darlin', oh my . . ."

Inside, Darby Buckingham felt his patience going; he wanted to choke the driver into gurgling silence. But he was trapped in the careening Concord stage and knew it, so he did what he figured was the next best thing. Pushing the window aside, he poked his head out to yell, but as the perpetual cloud of coach dust rose and engulfed him, he knew he'd made a mistake. The dust made his eyes water. Squinting them tightly and spitting dirt, he yelled up in a gravelly voice, "The first verse is, 'In a cavern, in a canyon, excavating for a mine, lived a miner, forty-niner, and his daughter Clementine!' Have you got that?"

The bearded face of Andy Carson emerged into his watery vision. "What's that you say, city man?"

Darby jerked his head back into the coach, gulped a cleaner breath, stuck it back out, and croaked the first stanza again.

"Thanks!" the driver hollered cheerfully.

Coughing and wheezing, Darby withdrew from the great outdoors and slammed the window shut. He began to mop his muddy, perspiring face and then listened.

"Oh my darlin', oh my darlin', oh my darlin' Clementine, you are lost and gone forever, dreadful sorry Clementine." There was a moment or two of silence, then, as Darby listened aghast: "Oh my darlin', oh my darlin' . . . dreadful sorry Clementine!"

Darby wondered if he would break his way through the roof of the stage to kill the driver. He hit it brutally hard with his fists; nothing gave but the skin over his knuckles. He gave up and promised himself revenge at the next stage stop.

"Here she comes," shouted a run-down-at-the-heels hostler as he drove a fresh team of horses into the stage yard. "Right on time, too!"

Two cowboys cast their smokes away, grabbed their bedrolls and saddles, and sauntered out to await the stage. As soon as it came to a stop, the tired, sweating team was unhitched and the new one snapped into the harness. "How'd ol' Strawberry pull today?" a man yelled. "He still up to his usual tricks?"

"Yep"–Andy grinned–"but I caught him a good one, once or twice."

"Sure ya did, Andy!" the man shouted good naturedly. "That roan has got your number; he knows a soft touch when he sees one."

The man leapt away as a familiar stream of juice came diving at him.

"More passengers?" Carson asked, looking at the cowboys.

"Yep," the hostler said, eying the driver suspiciously in case he was just being lured into range for a better shot. "These two men are going with you as far as Running Springs."

"Good," Carson said, snorting. Then, nodding toward the inside of the coach, he added, "I could use some company that appreciates good singing."

Darby heard the comment and chose to ignore it. He was in southeastern Wyoming now. It wouldn't be prudent, he realized, to thrash the bearded rascal who called himself a driver. More than likely, he'd have to take on the two hostlers and the rough-looking cowboys who were heaving their saddles up on the roof. It occurred to Darby that even if he did manage to overcome the lot of them, they wouldn't be disposed to take him on to Running Springs. Sinking darkly against the rocky cushions, he resigned himself to his predicament.

Once they were sure that their saddles and gear were secure, the men stepped up to the coach door and stared inside. Darby, in no mood for the social amenities, merely glared at them. The first cowboy, who had already placed a boot on the stage step, slowly withdrew it as the passengers regarded each other suspiciously.

"Think maybe I'll ride up top where I can get some fresh air," said the man to his partner.

"Suits me," came the offhand reply.

They closed the door and clambered up beside the driver.

"That city feller in thar, he looks plumb peeved over something," one of them remarked.

Andy Carson whipped the team and the Concord jumped into a high roll and went careening out of the station yard. "That feller, he just don't appreciate good singin' or the fine art of spittin', but I know you gents do. Oh my darlin', oh my . . ."

Several miles and hundreds of "Oh my darlin's" later, one cowboy poked the other and whispered, "Bert, I don't know how you figger it, but I'm beginning to understand why that city slicker looks so crabby. This driver's a spittin' fool; his aim is a purty thing to witness, but his singing is about to wear me down to a nubbin. I've heard some bad voices around night herd, but this feller tops it."

"For a fact," his partner replied. "And he don't seem to be running outa wind. I'd as soon hole up down below with that fat city slicker where we couldn't hear him so loud."

"Hey, driver, where do you figure that passenger of yours is headin'?"

"Said he was going to Running Springs, at least that's as far as his ticket takes him."

"A drummer, I suppose," speculated the man named Bert.

"Nope," Andy said. "Leastways he ain't carrying any sample cases with him."

"Makes a man curious why a dude like that would be going to a place like Running Springs. Driver, if you'd stop for a moment, we'd like to go down and ask him."

"Suit yourselves, cowboys, but you're going to miss out on a lot more good spittin' and singin'."

"Well," Bert drawled, "sometimes a man has to suffer some for his curiosity."

"Ain't that the truth," Andy Carson replied, pulling the stagecoach to a halt as the men gratefully leapt to the ground.

"Move over, mister. We're coming in to join ya."

Darby pushed his considerable bulk against the far door. "Plenty of room, gentlemen, plenty of room."

The man named Bert saw that Darby still took up three quarters of one seat. The one across from his was half full of mail sacks. "You better sit next to him, Wes. Yo're some skinnier than me."

Wes eyed the few inches of exposed cushion. "It would crowd a fat lizard to sit there," he grumbled, climbing in.

Darby heard the latter's remark and thought nothing of it. In fact, he mentally jotted the line down for use in an upcoming book. He was used to the kind of insult that a fat man receives. He'd carried extra baggage on his thick frame as long as he could remember. His father had always told him it had run in the Buckingham family, along with extraordinary strength. He had never heard of an underweight Buckingham and had no intentions of Darby starting the precedent. "With weight comes strength," he'd bristle ferociously. If there ever had been a slender Buckingham, the man would undoubtedly have been a weakling and a misfit, unworthy of his family name.

Darby had never known his mother; she had died during his first year of life, but he had pictures of her. Always, she was smiling hugely around plump cheeks and over layers of chins. Clearly, the late Mrs. Buckingham had not been worried about her weight.

Darby, too, had long since stopped being concerned about his waistline. It was his firm conviction that food and drink gave a man all his energies–this philosophy conveniently suited his life style. He loved steaks, ale, and whiskey; he wanted the best, and plenty of it. As far as he was concerned, if a feast left him a few ounces heavier, he was happy to pay the price. When men of lesser proportions found amusement in his appearance, that too could be easily settled–usually with his dark, ominous scowl, sometimes with more forceful efforts.

A first look at Buckingham was sure to leave an impression of harmlessness; a second or closer observation left a man wondering. So it was with the two cowboys named Bert and Wes. As soon as they were seated and found themselves enclosed with Darby, his dimensions seemed all the greater in comparison with their own.

Though both were of average size and weight, in the small coach each man somehow felt that he had shrunk. With the uneasiness upon them, it was Bert who spoke first. "No insult intended back there, mister."

Darby looked from one man to the other, decided they bore no malice, then reached into his coat pocket. "Would you gentlemen care to join me in smoking a cigar?"

Bert and Wes beamed. "Thanks, them's sure good-lookin' cigars, mister."

"Call me Darby," he said, striking a light for the three of them. "Do either of you know Sheriff Zeb Cather of Running Springs?"

"Old Zeb? Why hell, Mr. Darby, there ain't a man in this part of the country who don't know him."

Darby frowned, "You said 'Old Zeb.' How old is Mr. Cather?"

Bert shoved open the window and expelled a stream of blue-black smoke. "Oh, I don't know, what would you say, Wes?"

"Maybe sixty, I'd guess. I heard he was already a marshal down in Texas when he fought in the Colter-Barrow range war, and that must have been thirty, forty years ago."

"Yeah," Bert added, "he shot Barry Waco in the Colorado territory when I was still just a boy. We didn't hear about it till almost a year later, but I recollect it made folks talk."

"I remember that, too. It was said at the time that Waco was the best gun alive."

Darby sat and listened, trying to piece the story of Zeb Cather together. Finally, when Bert and Wes seemed about finished, he asked, "Why doesn't the sheriff quit and retire? Seems to me a man of sixty ought to learn to take life easier."

"You don't know Zeb. It ain't in his blood to sit back and play it safe. Besides, he's still the best man for the job."

"There's another reason," Bert added. "Old Zeb would never quit a fight, nor walk away from trouble."

Darby's attention focused. "What does that mean?"

"Just what I said. Right now there's trouble brewing at Running Springs. Trouble that's been a long time coming between Sheriff Cather and the Raton brothers. Though Zeb wouldn't admit it, most folks who know the situation think he has finally been pushed into more than he can handle. It seems to me he's up against a stacked deck."

Darby cursed silently to himself. Without even having met Sheriff Cather, he already felt personally involved in the trouble; he wished the stage would go faster.

Chapter 6

They were rolling a high dust sixty miles east of Running Springs when the right front wheel left the coach. Inside, Darby was thrown heavily onto Bert, causing the cowboy to let out a muffled cry of anguish. Overhead, they could hear Andy Carson, and he wasn't singing "Clementine." "Whoa, whoa! Damn you jugheads!"

The stage yawed heavily, struck axle, and came to a furrowing, grinding halt. Inside, Darby worked to uncover Bert; through the curtains, the prairie rose up before him. After several difficult moments, they finally managed to extricate themselves through the upward door. The first thing they heard was Andy Carson's swearing.

"A hell of a fix we're in now," Andy stormed, "but at least the axle didn't split, and it's a wonder. When I felt the wheel go, I jerked to the left. If the horse hadn't been savvy, I'd have rolled the whole durned rig on her back. Don't see how in tarnation we're gonna git that wheel back on. Maybe if we unload all the baggage and the government mail, we can lighten up enough to lift her, but I doubt it."

"Well," drawled Wes, "reckon we might as well fetch the wheel and give her a try. We don't figure out somethin', it's gonna be a long time come supper."

They rolled the heavy iron wheel back to the emptied coach. Darby had taken off his coat and tucked up both sleeves.

"City man," offered the stage driver, "you'd better just stand back out of the way while me and these boys put our backs to it."

"But, really . . ."

"Naw, that's all right. You don't need to dirty yourself up none," Carson interrupted. "There ain't much room around that hub, and you'd make a helluva squish if we dropped her on ya!"

Wes and Bert moved low to the coach; Andy pushed the wheel in close. "When I holler, gents, give it all ya got. . . . Lift!" he yelled.

The two cowboys bent their backs and heaved with all their corded, range-toughened muscles. Shaking and quivering they strained with their entire bodies and the coach edged up in creaking protest.

"Just a few more inches–just a few more and we got her, boys," Andy grunted, as he shoved the wheel in closer. "Don't give up, just another inch . . . jest . . ."

As Darby watched, Bert's eyes seemed to get larger and appeared in danger of leaving his face. Beside him, Wes grew beet red and the veins rose on his neck. Then, with a terrible slowness, the big Concord began to settle. The two cowboys shot frantic looks at each other, then abandoned the effort and jumped back. The coach dropped quietly, even lower than before. Andy Carson stood holding the wheel and swearing in frustration and anger. Behind him, Wes and Bert lay gasping on the prairie.

"Maybe I should give it a try," Darby suggested.

"Maybe you should go for a walk," Andy snorted.

Before the two stretched-out, panting cowboys could make a similar suggestion, Darby moved to the axle, carefully placed his hands on the smooth, worn wood, and lifted. The coach went up as his neck went in. "Jesus, mister! Hang on, that's too high. Jest let her down a mite."

"Take your time, Mr. Carson, and let me know when it is at the proper height."

Wes stared at his friend, disbelief written all over his face, but the latter was gazing open-mouthed, eyes going from the Concord to the Easterner. "I don't believe it!" he muttered.

Fifteen minutes later, they were heading for the next town's blacksmith shop. Andy Carson was singing "Clementine," and, in deference to the city man, he was using the first verse.

Bear Flats was a small, weary, undistinguished-looking town that had long since given up hope of rivaling either Cheyenne or even its closest neighbor, Running Springs. In the six years since big Matt Peavey had sunk his life savings into a run-down livery stable and blacksmith shop, neither the business nor the population had grown so's a man could tell it. As the long seasons dragged by, Peavey had gone bitter and sour with his sense of failure. Each year he tried to sell out; each year there were fewer prospects in sight.

So it was, on this afternoon, that the awesome smith stood before his livery, angrily working an iron wagon rod over the fire. Occasionally he'd look up to check the sun, mutter an obscenity, and go back to pounding. "Damn stage is never on time!" he swore, bringing a hammer crashing down to the anvil. The man held the rod in his work-blackened left hand and alternated pumping the bellows and striking with the hammer. His anvil rang and its strident sound carried out to meet the stage that he awaited. Today Concord was the only possibility of outside money. He knew he was disliked by the crusty old driver and that the man would always drive for repairs to Running Springs whenever possible. But the stretch of land that brought them into Bear Flats was rugged and often it gave Andy Carson no choice but to stop over for fixing or the tacking on of a thrown horseshoe.

When the stage rumbled noisily into town, the blacksmith shut down the forge and let the coals die. What he observed made a satisfied smirk crease the lines around his mouth. "Ha!" he spat. The stage company was gonna pay plenty for his work today. A man deserved to do right by himself whenever he had the opportunity. Crossing his huge dirty forearms before his chest, he leaned heavily against the livery and waited. Let the old devil come to him a-scrapin' and askin'. With the near wheel wobbling like it was, the stage had been damn lucky to make it into town. He'd have to tighten the hub. Maybe more if he could get away with it. He'd run up the bill plenty.

Andy Carson pulled on the lines and drove the stage toward the livery. He could see the mule-sized form of Bear Flats' only blacksmith and he let tobacco juice fly to show his displeasure. "Whoa up there, team," he ordered, pulling the wobbling Concord up before the livery. He glared down at Matt Peavey and saw the smith's expression of triumph. Almost a minute passed before Andy forced out the words: "Lost a wheel back yonder. You think you can tighten it back on?"

Matt took the remark as the insult it was. "Hell yes, old man. I can fix it up as good as new." He walked over to the wheel and regarded it with undisguised pleasure. "But it won't be easy. Have to take the whole thing off, rework the hub . . . I dunno"–he smiled maliciously–"going to be a lot of work. It's going to cost you plenty, Carson."

"How much?"

"Well, cause it's you"–the blacksmith grinned, rubbing his whiskery face–"ten dollars."

"Ten dollars! That's robbery! It wouldn't cost me more than five in Running Springs."

"But you ain't in Running Springs. You're in Bear Flats and ain't that a shame." Peavey smirked, enjoying himself immensely.

Darby surveyed the burly man with distaste. What he was doing was apparent to them all. He turned to regard the town; it wasn't any of his business, what he wanted was to get to Running Springs as soon as possible.

"Seems like a lot of money for a job like that," Wes commented sarcastically.

The blacksmith whirled on the cowboy. "Who the hell asked you, mister!" he snarled, balling his calloused hands.

Bert stepped up beside his friend. "Don't reckon anybody needed to," he stammered, color coming up into his face.

"Never mind, gents," Carson sighed, climbing down from his seat. "Matt here likes bustin' up folks as well as he fancies taking advantage of 'em. We ain't got no choice and the company wouldn't take it any easier if it had to pay for your doctorin' on top of the ten dollars. Go ahead and fix the damn wheel; but make it fast–I got me a schedule to keep."

"Good. I knew you'd see things my way. Now let's get this mangy team of yours unhitched," he said, sauntering up to the lead horse.

Andy worked to loosen the traces. He was unstrapping the last of them when Matt Peavey reached up and yanked the lead animal's bit. The horse slung its head away in pain.

"Move, damn you!" Peavey swore, yanking again.

The animal reared back, stomping the lines and jamming the team into the Concord.

Andy Carson dove sideways to keep from getting trampled and when he came to his feet, he was fighting mad. "Take yore dirty paws off of him! No man's gonna treat a animal of mine thataway!" he stormed, charging in at the blacksmith.

Matt released the bit. He ignored the blood that came off onto his hand. He raised his palm and slapped Carson the same as he would have a bothersome fly. The blow caught Andy square in the face and sent him sailing backward two feet off the ground. He skidded into the dirt and lay still.

Darby Buckingham walked in on the balls of his feet, hands up, knuckles white. Matt Peavey laughed. "You want some of the same, fat man, I'll . . ."

Darby hit him with his mouth open and felt his fist break teeth. He could see the shock wave as it traveled through the man's entire length. With satisfaction he stepped back and let the blacksmith come to earth, then hurried over to help Andy Carson.

Matt Peavey lay in a pile of fresh horse manure–its moisture pressed into his back. He wasn't sure how it had happened, but he knew he was in for one hell of a fight. His fingers reached into his whiskers. "One broke, another loosened," he whispered. "I'll kill him!" On arms as big as boot tops, he came to his feet and charged the Easterner.

"Behind you!" Andy gasped.

The blacksmith's heavy thudding footfalls coincided with the driver's shout. In apparent ignorance, Darby ignored both warnings, but as he bent toward the driver, he silently counted the pounding steps. On the seventh thud, he dropped to his knees. He heard a surprised shout and felt Matt strike him in the side and go flying over.

Matt found himself back in the dirt for the second time. He didn't like it. His breath was already coming fast as he turned to regard Buckingham at eye level. "Are you gonna stand up and fight like a man?" he spat.

"I am at your service," Darby said, rising to brush the dirt from his pants and smiling in anticipation.

With his grimy chest heaving out of his sweat-stained shirt, Matt moved cautiously forward. He feinted with his left and caught a left between the eyes for his trouble. It made him dizzy but he came on, dogged, determined. His arms began to windmill; just one punch, he thought, and I'll put him away.

Darby was forced backward. He blocked two overhands, sidestepped another, then took a blow across the top of his head that made his ears ring. He ducked and felt air stir above him. Then he set his feet in the dirt and threw his entire body into a driving uppercut straight to Peavey's stomach. Overhead, he heard a deep gasp as the blacksmith sucked for wind that wouldn't come. Darby Buckingham stepped back and put his weight into a right cross. His knuckles crunched into the blacksmith's face. This time, Darby knew his opponent wasn't going to come up for more.

It was a long time before Peavey could croak. When he did, his voice shook with hatred. "Ya beat me, but you're gonna pay, mister. You and the rest can walk to Running Springs. I'll be damned if I'll fix that hub!"

Darby walked over to the iron wagon rod lying beside the anvil. It was cold now and hard. His face was thoughtful as he picked it up and returned to the man. Kneeling down beside him, he slid the rod under Matt's neck. Then with a tremendous effort that almost drew his body into a ball, he bent the iron around into a full circle.

The blacksmith's eyes grew round with fear as he stared at the joined ends lying on his chest.

Darby smiled at him. "Unless you want to wear an iron necklace the rest of your life, you'll fix the stage, and soon, too, for I am anxious to reach Running Springs."

Chapter 7

"Thar she is," boomed Andy, "next stop, Running Springs, Wyoming, and the Concord Saloon!"

Forgetting about the dust, Darby poked his head out the window for his first glimpse of the long-awaited town. He was not disappointed. Far ahead, the buildings huddled together as if to derive protection from the massive mountains against which they stood. Trees and grass ran down from peaks that were covered, even through summer, with snowpack. And in many places glistening threads of silver water jumped down the rocks to race upon the plateau. The sheer immensity of the scene moved Darby. It was totally different from any feeling he had ever experienced. In the cities man erected his tall buildings, built enormous bridges, and lived with a feeling of power over the elements. In the West it was altogether different. It seemed to Darby that the town of Running Springs knelt humbly before the vast western sky and the ragged mountains which consorted with it.

The two cowboys did not complain of the dust that rushed into the coach. Instead, they merely pulled their bandanas up over their noses and waited in silence.

Darby finally swung the window shut and said, "It's a beautiful . . . Good God! I almost asphyxiated you gentlemen!"

"That's all right, Darby. In our line of work we're used to eatin' trail dust," said Bert. "That Running Springs is sure enough a pretty site for a town. Those mountains are the tag end of the Tetons—some folks have traveled clear out here just to look at them. Can you believe that?" he said, shaking his head in amazement.

"Yes, I can. I've seen pictures of the Alps in Europe. Your mountains are every bit as beautiful."

The two cowboys smiled as though they'd been complimented personally. "Bigger than you'd expected, ain't it?" Wes said. "You got any more of those Cuban cigars?"

"Sure, I've got a whole case full . . ."

"No, one will do. What you say, Bert? I'll cut her in half and we'll smoke the hell out of it before we get to town."

Bert nodded in agreement and whipped out a wicked-looking pocketknife. Darby shuddered in disgust as he watched the long, rich cigar sawed in half. Well, he thought, that notion that Westerners could shave with their knives sure isn't true.

Holding up the two ragged, mutilated ends, Bert grinned. "Here, Wes, you take the front end, I'll take the butt end."

"Fitting that you do," Wes replied drily.

Before Bert could reply, Darby asked, "How are the accommodations in Running Springs?"

"As good as you'll find in Wyoming," Wes said expansively. "You'll want to stay at the Antelope Hotel; it's the only two-story building in town. They got a dining room that serves up as good a feed as you could ask for. The widow woman Beavers owns it. If you pay in advance and plan to stay for a long spell, she'll see that you get clean sheets once a month!"

Darby visibly recoiled in shock. "Once a month!" he roared.

"Yeah," Bert grinned, winking at his partner, "I knew that would impress you."

Darby began to laugh, and after a moment the cowboys joined in until the whole stage was fairly booming with the sound of it.

When the laughter had run out, Darby said, "Tell me what you know of Running Springs—some background if you will, and description."

"Well," Bert drawled, "it's different-looking than most cattle towns because it's built around a plaza, like the Spanish were partial to."

"What does the plaza contain?"

"Trees, just trees and grass," said Wes, puffing contentedly on his cigar. "It's a big thing, maybe fifty by a hundred yards, and they don't seem to use it for much, except in the summer."

"Why in the summer?"

"Cause them trees give a man some shade."

"Yeah," Bert interrupted, "it's off limits for horses, but they had a hell of a time keeping fellers from ridin' through it."

"Couldn't the sheriff stop them?"

"Sure, when he was awake, but he's got to sleep sometime, and the boys got so's they'd keep watches on him for each other."

Bert slapped his leg, laughing. "You should have seen 'em. They'd get a couple bottles of whiskey; once that was pretty near gone, and themselves with it, they'd take to their horses. You never seen anything like it before, the way them cowboys could play tag in that plaza. The idea was, all ya had to do was hit the other fella with the corked whiskey bottle; it didn't matter none where you got him, I always aimed for his back, some of those boys would get pretty rough–aimed for the head. Anyways," he continued, "every time you got struck, you could take a big swallow on the bottle. Trouble was, some of the boys would get so drunk they'd ride right up next to one another. Then they'd throw the bottle back and forth at each other till one of 'em knocked the other out cold."

"Yeah," Wes said; "it was some kinda show. The sheriff had to take a man to Cheyenne one time. He was gone for two weeks, and the games went on from mornin' till night. Every cowhand in the country was here. The bars did a landslide business selling bottles, and the doc had a steady stream of busted heads to patch; but the townsfolk, that was a different matter."

Blowing a stream of smoke out the window, Bert reminisced, "Most of 'em were mad as hornets. I'll have to admit the plaza was ground up some and full of empty whiskey bottles—but we'd have picked 'em up."

"Instead, though, they voted to fence the damned thing in, to keep the horses out." Wes added, "Crying shame, that's what it was. Some of the boys talked about marking off a patch in the aspens up above, but the idea sorta petered out."

"Too far from the saloons," explained Bert.

Darby's pen was moving as he gathered the story. "And now I suppose the fun is all over in the plaza?"

"Well, not entirely, it ain't," confided Wes. "A lot of the boys are partial to that plaza fence. When they've had too much to drink, likely as not they'll tie their ponies up to one of the poles and walk into the plaza for a shady siesta."

"What's wrong with that?"

"Oh, nothing! It's just that along will come some cowboys hell bent for leather, hollerin' and tellin' the world they've arrived. First thing you know, that fence would start flying as the horses tied to it would start jumpin' and pullin' at it."

"Never was a time was a bad as that last holdup."

"Holdup!" Darby exclaimed. "What happened then?"

Bert was nursing his cigar to a nub, holding it very carefully between two fingers; he solemnly explained, "They picked a bad day to rob the bank, as I remember. There were no less than three ranch crews in town, getting supplies, having a few friendly drinks. Then, of a sudden, we heard shots and ran out into the street, and you should have seen the commotion! Sheriff Cather is a-firing at those fellers and there must have been forty horses jerkin' at that log-pole plaza fence, just a-tryin' to get the hell out of the way. My oh my, you just should have seen that fence come apart! Flew six ways to Sunday. Horses were running, logs a-flyin' in every direction. I saw some pilgrim in a buckboard who had the misfortune to get caught in it. His eyes liked to jumped clean out of his head when he saw what was goin' on around him. He just threw up the reins and dove headfirst into the wagon trying to escape alive. Well, he did, but it was pitiful what them flyin' poles did to his wagon. When it was all over, there wasn't nothin' left but him in a pile of broken boards."

"Folks around here," Wes advised, "say that a man is more apt to get killed by that damned plaza fence than a shoot-out."

"For a fact." Bert nodded.

Andy Carson hauled in on the lines and dragged the six sweating horses into a trot. The stage rocked onto Main Street coming from the east and passed between the Dooley's Mercantile Store and the Bull Dog Bar. With little fanfare, it ground to a creaking halt before the big, many-windowed Antelope Hotel. Darby and the two cowboys gratefully climbed out and stood stiff-legged, looking the town over. The hotel, Darby saw, was a massive, ornately carved wooden structure. How long since it had been painted was a matter of apparent unconcern. White peeling patches gave it the appearance of an old man's gray head with an acute case of the scales. Apparently, Wyoming's seasons were not easy on things made of wood.

Without waiting for the driver to sing his last chorus of "Clementine," Darby began to unload his bags from inside the stage. That accomplished, he turned around to find that Wes and Bert had already unloaded his trunks and carted them into the hotel lobby. Darby smiled gratefully and extended his hand. The three ex-passengers shook warmly. "How about a couple more of those cigars, to show my appreciation for your company and help?"

"Nope," Bert said, shaking his head. "Me and Wes'll go back to chewing tobacco. It just would have been kinda messy in the coach is all."

Darby nodded in enthusiastic agreement. "I appreciate your restraint, and if I see you over at the Concord Saloon one of these evenings, I'll buy you a drink."

As Bert and Wes headed for the livery, Darby's eyes turned upstreet. A piano was playing in the saloon and he watched a couple of cowboys as they made their way out of its swinging doors and trooped down the hollow boardwalk. On the corner between the Concord and the Antelope Hotel, a formidable-looking adobe building crouched defiantly. Bars like rifle barrels braced its windows.

"Is that where I can find Sheriff Cather?"

Andy looked down from his high perch and nodded. "Yep," he said, smiling. "Mister, do you mind if I give you some friendly advice?"

"No, I'd be grateful for it."

"Well, I want to thank ya for what you did back in Bear Flats; I never seen the likes of a man who could fight like you. But if you aim to keep on wearing that derby, even the iron in your fists ain't going to help you from biting off more trouble than you can handle."

Darby scowled. "I'm not one to look for trouble with any man. Fact is, I try to avoid it."

"But that's what I'm a-tryin' to tell you! Every likkered-up cowboy in town will try and poke fun at those clothes of yours. I know you could handle yourself against most any man in these parts in a fair fight. But there are some who'd put a bullet through you once they figured they were losing a brawl. We don't pack six-guns for show around here, mister. Your fists are no match against a Colt revolver. Best thing you could do would be to strap on a gun, then go over to Dooley's Mercantile and outfit yourself in a new set of duds—especially a new hat!"

So that was the way of it, thought Darby. He slowly drew a cigar out of his silk vest pocket, then nipped off the tip and lit it. Feeling Andy's critical look boring in on him, he returned his gaze upward. "Thanks for the advice. But I'm afraid I can't accept it. These clothes and this hat were handmade for a perfect fit, as are the other suits I have with me. Even if I were inclined to don your western garb, I couldn't do so. In all of New York, there are very few stores that can properly fit me—I doubt very much if Dooley's Mercantile would even attempt to try."

Andy sighed. "Well, don't say I didn't warn you, friend." Reaching down to shake hands, he added, "If I'm around and ya need help, just holler loud and clear."

Wes and Bert stood watching as Darby made his way into the hotel. Hoisting his saddle, Bert said, "That Darby fella, he's got a lot of sand."

"Too much," said his partner. "He should have taken old Carson's advice. The first time he comes across the Raton brothers, he's in for more trouble than he ever thought about having. Wearing those city clothes and that derby . . ." The cowboy shuddered as though he could see the spectacle. "Maybe if it comes down to a gunfight, we can help him out. He's going to need it."

Bert shook his head skeptically. "I don't know. I never seen a man who could hit like that."

"Not even Ernie Raton?"

"Well, maybe Ernie," Bert admitted.

"Trouble is, like the driver said, against a .44 Navy Colt, he ain't got much chance."

Bert nodded. "Hope he knows enough to realize that."

"If he ain't got sense enough to change those city clothes and buy a Stetson to wear instead of that black derby hat . . . well, I don't give the poor fellow long for this world," Wes said.

"Maybe we *should* have taken another cigar. If he gets plugged, he won't even have a chance to smoke 'em."

Chapter 8

Darby Buckingham pushed in at the door of the sheriff's office. It swung heavily, creakily, as the room opened. At the far end, facing the door, a man sat behind an old desk and he held a Navy Colt that was aimed at Darby's chest.

"You got business here, mister?" the man said, laying the pistol down softly and eying his fat, startled visitor with a look of amusement.

"Is that the way you greet visitors?"

"Yep. A man can't be too careful."

The two men eyed each other frankly. Zeb Cather's face didn't betray his age. It was tanned dark brown but scarcely wrinkled; yet, his hair was shot with gray and his eyebrows and mustache were predominantly white. Massive protruding cheekbones nearly succeeded in dominating a set of pale ice-blue eyes.

"I can't believe you came over here to glare at me," the sheriff said.

"No, I didn't, Sheriff Cather. I apologize for bursting in here without knocking and then staring at you like that. But to me you are sort of a curiosity."

"You're becoming one to me, too, mister. I think maybe you'd better state your business."

With characteristic directness, Darby said, "My business is you, Mr. Cather. I would like to write a book on your life." Seeing the slowly spreading frown, Darby pushed on: "It would be an honest book, no exaggerations. I know enough about you to believe I wouldn't need to invent anything."

"Mister, if you came clear out to Wyoming to write about me–I'm afraid you're in for a disappointment. I ain't interested."

"Mr. Cather, there are plenty of people who'd be interested in your story. I'd like to write it the way you've lived. Sooner or later, with your reputation, somebody is going to write about you. I offer you the chance to see that it is done honestly."

The sheriff picked up the worn, efficient-looking Colt and considered the gun carefully. "What you say may be true–but you came at the wrong time. Right now, I've got my hands full and my pockets running over with trouble." Eying Darby keenly, he added, "Anyone around me would be riskin' a bullet. And you'd be a hard target to miss, Mister . . ."

"Buckingham, Darby Buckingham."

"For another thing, Mr. Buckingham, I figure you're going to cause me some trouble walking around town all duded up like that. I ain't got time to watch out for you."

"I don't expect you to," Darby snorted.

The sheriff smiled. "No offense, Buckingham, but if I were you, I'd get on the next stage headin' out."

"Not until I have your story. If forced to, I'll get it from people in town, and other places you've been."

"You're a determined cuss, ain't you?" Zeb Cather said, reaching into his pocket for the makin's. "Look, I'll think it over. But I got trouble to settle and I can't be worrying about you getting hurt."

"I can take care of myself, Sheriff."

Zeb Cather looked at the man before him and smiled condescendingly. "Sure you can. I'll think on your offer. Now, if you'll excuse me."

"One thing, Sheriff. I've heard about a family named Raton. I'd like to know the nature of your trouble with them."

"The Ratons are choking this town, Mr. Buckingham; and,

unless they're stopped, they'll kill it with their cattle rustling, murdering, and land grabbing."

"Why haven't you put them behind bars?"

The sheriff smiled. "It ain't that easy . . ."

"I don't imagine stopping a range war was either."

"You've done some homework, haven't you, Mr. Buckingham?"

"Yes. I know some of the things you've done in Texas, Colorado, and Montana. That's why I don't believe you've lost your nerve in the face of this."

The sheriff chuckled, lit his cigarette, and said, "I'm grateful for the vote of confidence. Fact is, though, a few folks around here would say different. I'm not afraid of the Ratons. Probably should be, but I'm not. Maybe I've lived through so many shoot-outs I'm getting careless, but I'd have had a showdown long ago if I'd been able to get enough evidence on them to get a hangin'. Once I'm able to obtain the proof that they're behind this county's trouble, I'll go after them. Before I do, however, I'll write the marshal and court in Cheyenne and present my evidence. If they agree, it won't matter what happens to me—cause the Ratons'll swing."

Darby shook his head in wonderment. "It's a lot more than just going gunning for them, isn't it?"

"Hell yes, it is! You Easterners think we have no law out here; you're wrong. The days of outlaws and gunslingers riding roughshod over the land are gone. In places where the law doesn't handle justice, vigilante committees will spring up and do the hangin'. I've never had a vigilante committee in a town of mine—never want to. Often enough, they string up a few innocent people along with the guilty. No," he said, picking up a wanted poster and staring at it, "if I got proof, they'll swing, whether I'm around to watch it or not!"

"How many are there, Sheriff?"

"There's the old man, mean as a rattler. He's got three grown sons with him. Each of them handles a gun like he was born with it—which they probably all were. If you see them in town, head for cover. You'll know them cause they are all tall, big-boned redheads, except for the old man, his hair is whiter than mine. Also, they ride horses bearing the Circle R brand. If they're in town, you'll see their horses tied up in front of one of the saloons–stay out of it."

"You need help," Darby said simply.

"Sure I do, Mr. Buckingham, but you aren't the one to give it."

Darby opened his mouth to differ, but closed it instead. Words, he knew, would not convince anyone; they never had. "I'll be staying at the Antelope Hotel. I hope you'll reconsider."

Sheriff Zeb Cather watched Darby as he rolled heavily down the groaning boardwalk. A funny bird, he thought. Sort of liked him–built like a cannonball. Hope he stays in his room and out of the saloons; otherwise, some cowboys are gonna have a fine time with him.

Darby met the widow woman Beavers. She was overdressed and heavily rouged. High, greasy eyebrows peered at his prosperous appearance and Darby had the feeling he was being measured up for a meal. "Well, hello there, mister," she cooed, moving close.

Darby, reacting to the thick, sickening smell of cheap perfume, retreated and quickly drew out a cigar.

"My name is Dolly Beavers, and I own this hotel. It ain't often I have a gentleman like yourself rooming with me. How long will you be staying, big boy?"

Puffing like mad, Darby muttered something indefinite and screwed his face up into his most fearsome scowl.

"Whatcha frowning for, honey? Don't your cigar taste good?" Then, before he could reply, she walked over to the desk and examined a big board of huge keys. "Let's see," she said, musing, "yes, yes, I think I can let you have it. Really, Mister . . ."

"Buckingham, Darby Buckingham."

"Really, Mr. Derby, you are very lucky. The Hickok room is available."

"The Hickok room?"

"Yes. Maybe you've heard folks call him 'Wild Bill.' He slept here once–and now he's famous."

"Is it your best room, and does it look out over the main street?" he asked, unimpressed.

"Why of course," she said, sounding slightly offended, "and it's right next to mine. In case you need anything, Mr. Buckingham, you only need to pound on the wall, and I'll be right over, day or night."

The cigar went bad in his mouth; it had never happened before. "If you'll give me the key, Mrs. Beavers, I'll go up to my room."

"Call me Dolly, and I'll call you Derby."

"Darby! D-A-R-B-Y," he spelled out loudly.

"Of course, honey, right this way. I'll show you your room."

It was clean, but spartan. After he finally ushered Mrs. Beavers out, the writer sat on his bed and looked forlornly around the room. There were faded rugs of undeterminable color, a scarred washstand and dresser, and the brass bed upon which he sat. Above the bed someone had carved "Arnie Wafers slept here too." For a few moments, Darby seriously considered returning to New York. He thought longingly of his desk, books, and the luxurious apartment at 117 Plaza Street, and wished he had taken his publishers' advice and stayed. The room depressed him almost as much as the thought of Mrs. Beavers being right next door. He thought about going down to eat, but realized he wasn't hungry. That was bad, he decided; when a Buckingham lost his appetite, things were indeed bleak. Perhaps some fresh air would help. Languidly, he moved to the window and opened it. Darby looked out into the street and over the plaza. Instantly, he forgot about his apartment in the city and his loss of appetite. For coming down the center of Main Street, as though they owned it, rode two mean-looking young men. Hats pushed back, their thick red hair streamed down over their ears and lay plastered to their foreheads. They rode horses branded with a Circle R, and they rode them loosely, as their eyes went from store to store, stopped on the sheriff's office, then moved on to the Concord Saloon.

Darby watched the two men tie up and saunter through the swinging doors of the saloon. He pulled the drapes shut and moved back into his room, then began to pace back and forth, lost in deep thought.

The sheriff, unless something prompted him to think otherwise, would not consent to letting the book be written. Darby knew that he cut a poor figure next to most men, and Zeb Cather had sized him up no differently than had anyone else he'd met west of the Missouri so far. Ordinarily that did not concern him, but with the sheriff it was a different matter. Something had to be done to change the sheriff's mind. Darby knew of only one thing that might do it. The trouble was, it might cost him his life.

He was about ready to leave the hotel; he had changed into his oldest suit, and the shirt he liked least. After several minutes of consideration, he left his tie; it made too easy a noose. Before he stepped out into the hall, he carefully set the round black derby on his head. Staring at himself in grunting approval, he left the room—he was heading for the Concord, to pick a fight with the Raton brothers.

Chapter 9

The hot sun was fading and people were beginning to move out into the late afternoon coolness when Darby stepped from the Antelope Hotel. It was the best time of day in Running Springs and the dimming light was kind to the Wyoming town. Carefully preparing a cigar, he decided to start eastward and travel around the entire circumference of the plaza and finish up at the Concord Saloon. The walk around the town, he felt, would serve several purposes. If he were to write about Zeb Cather, he knew he would have to understand the kind of people and life the town held—to get a feeling for it. Also, after the long hours of stagecoach confinement, it would do him good to get the exercise and regain his appetite. But, most important, he wanted the Raton brothers to have time for a few drinks before he reached the saloon. Darby Buckingham wished them to be in a playful mood when he arrived.

The bank wasn't much to look at, and already it was closed for the day. Dooley's Mercantile was another matter. From the rafters to the floors, linens, ropes, dry goods, suits, pants, and barrels of crackers and flour mixed into an enormous assortment of everything.

Peering through the dirty front window, Darby could see a thin, balding man in an apron waiting on an attractive middle-aged woman. In the far corner, a small boy stood staring up at a big poster that extolled the merits of a chewing tobacco. Not wishing to interrupt in the middle of a sale, Darby cut across the street and peeked over the swinging doors of the Bull Dog Bar. It was inhabited by just three bored-looking cowboys nursing their beers, and an even more bored-looking bartender.

"Would ya look at that!" exclaimed one of the cowboys. Immediately, all heads swung to the front doors. With only his eyes showing, about all they could see of Darby was his round black derby. Quick as could be, the first cowboy drew his gun out and sighted in on the hat. Darby jumped to one side as the bullet shot out over the doors and climbed up over the plaza; then he moved quickly down the boardwalk.

"Hey," yelled the man, emerging from the Bull Dog. "I was just funnin' a mite. Come on back and I'll buy you a drink!"

"One thing for certain," laughed a grinning cowboy; "you sure didn't hit him; he's movin' too good!"

Farther down, he passed the hardware store and a restaurant, thinking how good the advice of everyone he'd met concerning his hat had been. He didn't fear a walking man when it came to a fistfight, but if every drunk cowboy in Running Springs was going to take potshots at him, then he was in for more trouble than he'd expected.

He was approaching the Bent Bucket Saloon, and his first thought was to duck his head and move by fast; but then he stopped. If he ever intended to stay in this town long enough to get his story, he had to make his stand sooner or later—and, he realized, the sooner, the better. Drawing a deep breath, he decided he'd like a beer and marched inside, expecting the worst.

The Bent Bucket was a long, narrow saloon, not wide enough even for tables. At the far end, leaning on the bar, two cowboys turned to watch Darby as he entered.

"My oh my! Would you just look at that hat!" one said, coming upright. "I'd sure like me a hat like that one." Elbowing the man beside him, he said, "Wouldn't you like a hat like that, Willard?"

"Yeah, for a fact I would," slurred his grinning friend.

"Then let's try it on!" replied the first.

In the sudden dimness of the bar, Darby Buckingham stood staring at the two rocking cowboys as they approached. Pushing the derby down firmly, he moved forward and met then just as the first one called, "Hey, Willard . . ."

Darby leapt, hands outstretched to grab the cowboy's shirt. Wadding some in each fist, he drove his body forward and shoved the two startled men into a reeling, momentum-gaining backstep. With a tremendous crash, they barreled into the rear of the saloon. Boards tore, splintered, and two cowboys blew through the back wall and cartwheeled into a rear alley.

Standing just in front of the ragged hole, Darby could clearly see the two squirming cowboys as they lay outside on an uneven bed of scattered timber.

"Jeezus, mister!" the bartender swore from behind. "They was only fixin' to have a little fun!"

"At my expense."

"Yeah, but . . ."

"This saloon needed a back exit, and it needed airing out—now you have both," Darby said, smiling expansively.

"Who the hell are you?" the bartender demanded incredulously.

"Name is Buckingham, Darby Buckingham, and I'm pleased to meet you, sir."

"Well, you sure have a hell of an entrance, mister," the bartender grumbled, frowning at the hole in his wall.

Darby turned back toward the alley. The two men were beginning to show signs of renewed life. "What were those gentlemen drinking?"

"Ya mean Willard and Hank?"

Darby nodded.

"Beers."

"Then I'll have three beers," he said, reaching for his wallet.

The bartender poured the beers and Darby carried two back to the gaping hole.

"Would you men care to join me in a beer?" he said, setting the glasses on the floor and extending his hand through the boards. "My name is Darby Buckingham, and I'm new here in Running Springs."

Hank rubbed his whiskers and stared unblinkingly at the Easterner. "Derby Man, I reckon we'll just take you up on that. Come on, Willard, let's join him in a beer."

Willard came through the wall, rubbing a place on the back of his head where a knot was already starting to emerge. "Nice looking hat you got there, Derby Man," he said, grinning sheepishly.

An hour and several beers later, Darby emerged from the Bent Bucket Saloon and passed around the plaza toward the noisy Concord. The light was almost gone, but he could see that two horses were still tied to the hitching rail. The only trouble was, in the darkness he wasn't convinced they were the Ratons' horses. He eyed them intently and they returned his look, snorting spookily. He considered going to them and feeling for their brands, but rejected the idea. Well, he reasoned, only one way to find out for certain. Ramming his hat down squarely, Darby Buckingham went to take a look at Running Springs' most popular saloon and the Raton brothers.

His generous stomach churned anxiously as he pushed between the creaking batwing doors. Once inside, Darby felt as if he had been transformed into some kind of circus oddity—the way the entire barroom turned to look at him. At two faro tables, the dealers stopped in midmotion. The first person to move was the florid-faced, sweating bartender, who hurried down toward him with a worried look. A look that shouted a warning.

"Leave him stay, Carl!" hollered a man at the bartender as he passed. Carl froze and moved away from the redhead. "Don't hurt him, Ernie. I'll . . ."

Ernie ignored him and left his place at the bar to see the newcomer.

Darby wished he'd stayed in the Bent Bucket with Hank and Willard—but he was committed, so he walked over to the smooth, polished bar. "I'll have a beer," he said quietly.

One redhead had become two—both wore smiles that were somehow not the kind that made you feel all friendly inside.

"Well, what do you know," leered the man called Ernie to his look-alike. "Just see what we have here, and just when I thought we were going to have to be content with teasing old Everett."

"Sure enough looks like we got a real live attraction here tonight, all dressed up like some kind of polar bird."

"Hey, Carl, did you hire this here fat man so's we'd ease off ol' Ev tonight?"

The bartender sidled closer to Darby, pity on his face. "Mister, I think you'd better leave. For God's sake, run for the door!" he whispered.

"Shut your mouth, Carl! Me and Jeb are gonna have some fun with him."

"Come on, Ernie," pleaded the bartender, "let him go."

Ernie grinned. "Hell, are you crazy? The man here wants his beer; go ahead and give it to him. He's gonna buy us a couple, too. He looks prosperous and hawg-fat to me, don't he to you, Jeb?"

"Sure does," the younger one said, reaching out and jabbing the writer in the side.

Darby stood facing the bar, knuckles white and close against his chest. "Go ahead, Carl," he said; "pour those beers on me."

"That's the stuff, dude!" the older brother laughed and slapped Darby hard on the back. From a distance, it might have passed as a gesture of good-natured overexuberance, but Darby knew better. Just before the man had slapped him, he had balled his fist, and he drove it into the soft flesh between Darby's shoulder blades. The blow was intended to flatten the Easterner, but he stood fast as though he hadn't felt it. Ernie stepped back, disbelieving.

"Here are your beers, mister," Carl said. Then he added in a quick whisper, "Run for the sheriff's office, stranger!"

"Thank you," said Darby, ignoring the advice and lifting a mug in each hand. Turning to face the two Raton brothers, he quickly sized them up and decided they were bigger than he'd first guessed. Especially the older one, named Ernie, who stood an inch and twenty pounds more than his six-foot-three-inch brother.

They grinned at him. Jeb winked knowingly at Ernie, then giggled.

"To your health–may it fail," Darby monotoned as the two Ratons reached out with big, red-freckled hands.

Darby flipped the two heavy mugs up hard, and the foamy sheets of beer caught them both full in their leering faces. Instantly, before the first enraged oath, or even before the first frothy drop had hit the floor, Darby punched the bigger man. His fist traveled only a foot, but he connected so solidly that Ernie went careening over a faro table as though he'd been mule-kicked.

Jeb jerked a hand across his face, spluttering and blinking; the first thing he saw was a set of flat knuckles boring in at a spot between his eyes. A second later, he felt a huge throbbing in his skull and discovered that he was stretched on the floor. Disbelievingly, he lifted and shook his head to clear the vision and his eyes came to rest on the bloody, slack expression of Ernie. It seemed to take a moment for Jeb to realize what had happened. With his hands spaced wide, he focused on Darby. Comprehension rushed in and he hissed, "Let's kill that fat bastard!" Beside him, Ernie nodded and pushed himself to his knees. He stared vacantly at the blood which dripped from his nose and soaked the planks.

Darby waited for them and absently surveyed his flat, tissue-scarred, fighter's knuckles. As usual, the right one, coming first and catching Ernie, had been the best. The left hadn't been as effective, and Jeb was recovering first. He looked around at the crowd–they seemed frozen, caught in the middle of expectant smiles that seemed in danger of melting.

Someone was half laughing, half crying. Darby turned to stare at an unshaven, sallow-faced man who rocked drunkenly back and forth. He lay between a couple of chairs near the front swinging doors. The old cowboy wore a beat-down hat and he was covered with tobacco-juice stains. Around him were a few scattered silver coins. Instinctively, Darby knew the drunk was there for sport, and to beg–money or tobacco juice, whichever suited a man's mood. He knew before thinking, it was the one they called 'old Everett.'" A human wreckage that was a perverse attraction for the likes of men such as Ernie and Jeb Raton.

"You hit 'em!" the drunk cried. "You hit 'em like I never saw a man hit, and . . ." The words trailed off but were stifled in sobbing for only a moment. "Look at 'em, the mighty Ratons–trying to get off the floor, same as old Ev. Jest the same as ol', no-good Ev . . ."

Darby Buckingham's throat went tight and he swung away from the man. He watched Jeb yank his brother erect.

They came then, Jeb fast and grim, not badly hurt and intent on killing; Ernie cautious, just wanting to maim.

Jeb swung a fist, his young, hard muscles unsnapping an overhand right that swept off Darby's hat and left the side of his face numb. His momentum threw him into Buckingham, pinning him. The bar dug and sawed at Darby's back as he fought to get free from Jeb's bear hug. Overpowering the man, he broke his right arm loose and poked a desperate jab at the onrushing Ernie. But it only slowed the man down for a moment and then they were both on him, and Darby reverted to instinct as they crashed to the floor.

Everett watched as they took Darby down. He was drunk and sick, but he fought to get up. He clawed at the chairs, table and window sill, and it seemed to him that he wanted, more than anything, to help the hard-hitting Easterner who dared to wear a derby and strike back against a Raton. They got him down, gotta help . . . they'll kill him for hitting them like he did, he thought. Everett ripped off a fingernail scratching for a handhold, but he came up and staggered through the front doors, trying to move fast but feeling all disjointed and fallen apart. "Sheriff! Sheriff!" he croaked into the night. "Help, they're gonna kill him sure!"

Darby battled to his feet–came up like a mountain with Jeb clinging to his back and Ernie swinging with every sinewy pound he had in his fists. The writer's left eye was puffed closed and his mustache dripped blood from a split upper lip. Jeb was straining, trying to choke him from behind. But Darby's neck, what little there was of it, was like the trunk of a tree and he kept his chin down. So Jeb couldn't get his choke hold, despite the weight of his whole body concentrated on his muscle-corded forearm. He could see Ernie giving a punch and taking a worse one, and he swore in helplessness. Only a short distance from his free hand he saw a half-full bottle of whiskey; he strained to reach it.

Ernie Raton stepped back, his face was cocked into a queer angle from a broken cheekbone and his breath whistled lispingly through holes where his two front teeth had been. Jeb, he saw, was trying to reach a bottle, and so Ernie sidestepped and feinted to his left. Then he stepped back and watched Darby lean to his right to block the punch–it brought the bottle into Jeb's reach.

Ernie should have waited for his brother to use the whiskey bottle, but he didn't. Instead, he gathered himself and threw a punch that carried every ounce of strength he had left. It came in like a freight train, and, trapped against the bar with Jeb all over him, Darby couldn't stay out of its way. A blocking forearm only succeeded in angling the fist into the side of his jaw. He felt his legs buckle and fell forward into Ernie's knees, carrying the bottle-waving Jeb Raton down on top of him. Twisting hard, he scraped over onto his back–Jeb hollered and let loose. With the man's weight suddenly gone, Darby surged to his feet. Ernie Raton was waiting for him spraddle-legged; he had measured the distance and put his body behind a chopping, overhand right. It caught Darby high on the cheekbone; he reeled backward into the bar, shaking glasses along its entire polished length. Darby's head spun and he twisted from side to side, ducking and dodging Ernie's punches, trying to see an opening. The bigger Raton threw all caution aside as he strove for a finishing blow, and he left himself open. Darby saw it and reacted instinctively with a blurring left hook to the apex of Ernie's rib cage. Ernie's breath blasted outward with a whoosh as his mouth gaped open. In agony, his big body strained upward onto his toes. Stretched out to his full six feet four inches, Ernie never even saw the straight right cross that slammed him senseless into the beer-mud on the barroom floor.

Darby turned, wanting to finish it but doubting if he had the strength. From the corner of his eye he caught the high, amber glint of the downward arching whiskey bottle. Jeb had it by the uncorked neck and the liquid gurgled wetly out onto his shoulder as he brought it down in a full circle toward the Easterner's head. Even as he saw it coming, Darby knew he would never have time to stop it–to get out of its way–and he closed his eyes.

A roar shook the room as the bottle came apart in Jeb's hand, glass and whiskey showering. Darby heard the gunshot and felt the wet spray and wondered if someone was shooting at his back.

"Hold it, Jeb! It's over. You boys goaded the wrong man tonight–you should have stuck to tormenting Ev here," Zeb Cather said sarcastically, as his free hand supported the drunk.

With the whiskey running from his head and down his face, Jeb Raton glared red-eyed at the gun in the sheriff's hand. "It ain't over! Damn you, Zeb! Look at what he did to Ernie. He blame near killed him. He owes us!"

"Yeah," the sheriff said, looking at the scarcely recognizable brother. "Looks to me like he paid you what you had coming. Now pick him up, Jeb, and get him outa here before I jail you both!"

Jeb spat, "You're gonna pay for this, Sheriff. Ain't no getting around it now. Once Pa sees Ernie, he's gonna want to even a score with you for siding with that city slicker. He'll see you dead, only he'll make you sweat awhile, wondering when. And you," he said, eying Darby, "when Ernie comes around, it'll be with a gun–same as me!"

They moved out to their horses, Jeb bent over and hurt, his brother carried by three straining cowboys. Darby stood beside Everett and the sheriff. Most of the town had already heard of the fight and gathered staring in awe at the battered Darby Buckingham. But worse still was the mess called Ernie Raton–a man who had never been whipped to anyone's recollection until tonight. He left Running Springs tied over his saddle.

Zeb Cather shook his head in disbelief and watched Darby search for a cigar. "You know, you almost got brained. If old Ev here hadn't come hollering into my office, Jeb would probably have killed you with that bottle."

Through a crack in his one unclosed eye, Darby looked at Ev. "You, of all the people in here, helped me. I don't understand why."

The watery, bloodshot eyes bored at him. "I never saw anyone hit Ernie like that–it's always been the other way around, likely as not me, if I'm standing. It was better than a drink to see a Raton down on the floor. Mister, you don't owe old Ev any favors. What you did to the Ratons here tonight ain't going to be forgotten, especially by me."

"Nor Ernie," said the sheriff. "He'll come gunning for you as soon as he's able. There'll be his brothers and the old man along with him. Take the morning stage out and live to write another book, Buckingham."

"It's your story I'm after. As long as we both have the same enemies now, I think we might as well work together. It seems to me we might even have a few things in common—besides mutual enemies, I mean."

The sheriff looked at the man before him. "Damned if I ever seen anything like you," he grinned. "Those Ratons mean what they say. This isn't just some yarn like you'd spin in one of your books."

"I know, Sheriff; it's better. And I intend to stay to see this thing out."

Darby turned toward Everett. "Have you been in Running Springs long?"

"What if I have?" the man asked.

"I'm going to need someone to fill me in on background—show me around. I'm willing to pay for your services, Mister . . ."

Ev seemed to rise slightly until he stood a little taller than Darby. "My family name was Randall, but most folks just call me old Ev."

"Well, Mr. Randall, are you interested in the proposition?"

Everett's fingers shook as they tried to brush some of the dirt from his ragged clothes. "I'll help you," he said. "I'd help the devil himself if he whipped Jeb and Ernie like you did."

Darby nodded approvingly. "Would you and the sheriff care to join me in a long-overdue beer?"

Old Everett's mouth flapped open, but he forced it to say, "Nope, reckon I'll just mosey on over to the livery and turn in. I had enough liquor, and for a change, I ain't of a mind to drink myself into forgetting tonight."

"I'll be calling for you from the Antelope Hotel, room number nine."

Everett started to tell the Easterner that Mrs. Beavers wouldn't allow him into the hotel, but he thought better of it.

Besides, he sort of felt that the man named Buckingham would change all that.

"And you, Sheriff," Darby said, touching a match to the one unbroken surviving cigar of the fight, "would you care to join me in a beer?"

But the sheriff was gazing after the retreating form of Everett Randall. "Funny," he mused; "first time in almost two years I've heard him refuse a drink."

Chapter 10

Darby Buckingham placed his beer softly on the bar and regarded the sheriff between rapidly swelling eyes. "Do you mean to say that Mr. Randall has been drinking steadily since then?"

"Yep, ever since that first night I rode into town with him after we came back from the Raton ranch. At first, he just drank mostly on the nights that Jeb or Ernie were in town. But, as the months went by, and we couldn't pin anything on them, he took to drinkin' more and more. Finally, about three months ago, I figured he ran out of money, cause the Widow Beavers threw him out of his room; now he sleeps at the livery, cleans stalls, and sweeps walks for his eatin' money."

"Have you tried to talk to him about the madness of his purpose? Surely he must know that he may kill himself before justice brings those two men to account."

The sheriff wearily nodded in agreement. "Every time I speak to him about it, he just asks me if I have any new evidence on the Ratons. So far, I haven't been able to tell him anything. He just says he'll keep drinking and listening until one of us gets evidence."

Darby looked down the bar, caught Carl's eye, and called for two more beers. The pain in his face was beginning to numb slightly; but, inside, thinking about Everett Randall, he felt worse. "If he hadn't gone for help, Sheriff, Jeb would have knocked me cold with that bottle."

"If he hadn't caved in your skull with the first shot, he'd have finished you with the next. I'd have been too late to help you," the sheriff said. "Hell, I was sitting at my desk cleaning a rifle when Everett came running through the door hollering about the derby man needing help. I didn't think he could still run like that. I guess I should have known he wasn't as drunk as he likes people to think, especially when Jeb and Ernie are drinking here."

The memory of the half-crying man, laying small and crumpled between the tables, came to Darby. The drunk old Everett was the only man in the Concord Saloon who'd helped him. "He wasn't sober, Sheriff, but he still had enough courage to go after you."

"When the time comes, he'll still have enough left to go after Jeb and Ernie, too," the sheriff said. "I guess he ain't got much; his money's gone, and so is his pride. But he still owns a horse and rifle. Sometimes, when he can, I see him ride out through the alley going toward the mountains. He don't come back until late, but I don't have to ask him where he's been."

"Mrs. Randall?"

"Yeah, her and the rifle and the revenge. They're all he's got left."

"I'd like to help him, Zeb."

"So would I. But there's only one thing that will keep him from drinking himself to death."

"And that is . . . ?"

"The day the Ratons pay for the thieving and killing they've done–with bullets or at the end of a rope."

Darby Buckingham smiled through split lips and knew the pain was still there. Picking up his beer, he eyed the sheriff and said, "I owe Mr. Randall a favor. I'm going to help you get the evidence you need to see they hang."

"How do you propose to do that?"

"I honestly don't know," Darby admitted, "but something will turn up sooner or later."

Finishing another beer, Darby yawned. "It has been a long first day for me in Running Springs. Good night, Sheriff. I'll look forward to beginning the work on your book tomorrow."

As he was about to leave, the sheriff grabbed the writer's sleeve. "Hell, Buckingham, I'll be glad to work with you if you're so all-fired set on writing my story. But as for Jeb and Ernie, they won't make the same mistake they did in here tonight. Next time, they'll use guns. Old Everett and I have a reason for wanting them hung, but you don't . . ."

"That's where you're wrong, Mr. Cather. I have as good a reason as either of you, now."

"What's that?"

"The Ratons won't let me get away with publicly humiliating them in here. They'll think about it while they heal their wounds; finally, when they're able, they'll try to kill me for the beating I gave them. My reason, Sheriff, is therefore very simple. It is them or me; and I prefer it to be them! Good night."

The rapping sound was getting steadily louder as Darby felt the beginnings of pain from the previous night's fight. As awareness hit him, he groaned and pulled the pillow over his head. Still the noise grew until, at last, he hurled the pillow at the door.

"Really, Mr. Buckingham!" she shrieked. "I was only bringing you some hot coffee. And now you've made me spill most of it," the widow said, watching the coffee slosh downward to soak wetly into the pillow.

"What time is it, Mrs. Beavers?"

"Oh, heavens, honey, how do I know? But the sun's almost full-up and . . ."

Darby growled menacingly and began to grope for a shoe to throw, but just as his fingers grasped it, she said, "Here, let me help you with that. Where are your socks, you strong man you. Really, Derby, the whole town is buzzing about how you thrashed Jeb and Ernie Raton last night. And I'm so proud of you!" she squealed, bending over and aiming a kiss at his forehead and missing.

"Ouch!" he screamed, grabbing his black swollen eye. Through the one partly good one, he glared redly at her. "Mrs. Beavers . . ."

"Call me Dolly," she said, slipping a hand under the covers.

"Really, Mrs. Beavers!" he exclaimed.

"Oh, Derby, I was only trying to grab your arm and feel that big strong muscle of yours. Anyone who could . . ."

Darby groaned. "Please, Mrs. . . . Dolly, please give me what's left of the coffee and leave so I can go back to sleep."

A shadow of disappointment passed across her face, but was gone before he could say more.

"Oh, all right, Derby, honey, I guess I'll let you sleep in today because of last night. But after this, I'll expect you to have breakfast with me. Bye now!" she breathed, backing toward the door; "bye now!"

Sheriff Cather leaned back in his desk chair and absently sighted his Colt on a fly that was walking across the ceiling. "The truth is, Darby, I don't know what you're interested in hearing. I've lived sixty-two years and that's quite a yarn to stretch out."

"Just start at the beginning, Sheriff. As you talk, I'll be writing notes and episodes that will later be pulled together in your book. We'll start by working just a few hours a day; after you get used to it, you'll probably forget I'm even here."

Zeb Cather let his mind drift back over the years past, when he was a young man and even back to his childhood that seemed a long time gone. "I was born on a ranch in southeastern Texas. My maw died when I was just five, so I don't remember much of her. Mostly, it was just Pa and my brother and never enough grass or water. We had a few head of horses and some half-wild longhorns and we managed to eat at least once a day. We worked hard, but they were good times up until I was twelve years old. . . ."

Darby's pen flew over the paper, sometimes hesitating for a moment, catching a word or phrase, then rushing on to gather the thread of a man's life.

A thin boy, all patches and angles, rode a splayfooted dun carefully through the heavy brush. He held an ancient, long-barreled flintlock rifle, which rocked with the steady motion of his horse. It pointed skyward toward a late afternoon sun which was blazing out heat in a last searing effort to drain the juices of anything that moved beneath it. Young Zeb Cather squinted and rubbed at the salt sweat that burned his eyes. Draped limply over the horse's withers dangled two stringy rabbits that hung softly before his knees. Blood still dripped from the mouth of one, and occasionally a drop would splash upon the boy's boot and sink darkly into the rough, dusty leather.

But Zeb paid no attention, for his eyes were hard on the land before him, and especially the ridges that heaved up ahead towards where he had to ride to reach the sod dugout they called home.

He pulled his horse in and listened; there were sounds, but they were safe sounds—a bird cutting through the brush, the scurrying, rapid thumpings of a rabbit, but that was all, and that was good. For his older brother, Billy, had seen the Comanches only a week earlier, and today was the first time his father had allowed the boy to move away from the house to hunt. Zeb's heels drummed hollowly on the empty belly of the horse, and together they moved forward.

It was very quiet as he reined out of the dry gravel wash and picked a faint game trail that ran towards higher ground. Beyond it, he knew, a slope fell towards a spring that gave life to grass and willows. Near the spring, poking outward toward the meadow and dug back into the earth, crouched their dugout.

Twenty feet from the top of the rise, he stopped and dismounted; as he landed, his heavy boots kicked up puffs of dust. He flipped the reins over the horse's head and tied them quietly to a piece of brush. As he moved forward, the dun waited, head down, and the dead rabbit continued to drip.

He came to the summit and crouched low to the earth. In sharp contrast to the dry brush-covered rise upon which he lay, the meadow below lay cool and green clear up to the opposite side where the dugout was barely visible. He could see Billy leaning on an ax handle, and before him the new-cut whiteness of cottonwood shone like fresh snow in the morning sunlight. His father was walking up from the stream, carrying a bucket in each hand, and Zeb watched as water sloshed brightly over their edges.

The boy saw the Indians almost as his father stretched up into the air and the pails smashed to earth, sending the water to darken the soil onto which he toppled.

"Pa!" he screamed across the distance. Almost as though his father had heard him, the rancher rose and fired as three mounted Comanche warriors burst from the willows. His gun cracked and one rider flipped backward, throwing a lance toward the sky. The other two Indians raced down upon him, and, as they passed over, Zeb could see his father on the grass and Billy running for the house.

Zeb screamed in frustration and the agony of his helplessness. He watched as Billy slammed the door. A lance buried itself in the wood where the opening had been. Zeb didn't wait to see more; sobbing and cursing, he started back for the dun. As he ran, he checked the long rifle even though he knew it was ready. When he came down the slope minutes later, Zeb could see a riderless horse running away, and two Comanches smashing at the dugout's door. He was still forty yards distant when the wood gave way and one of the Indians hurled himself into the interior that belched black powder smoke and gunshots; the other Indian was yanking the buried lance off the door. "No, no!" he cried, "Hang on Billy, I'm coming!" He kicked off the dun as it swept through the front yard. Its momentum sent him sprawling face first into the dirt as a war lance silently cut the air where his body should have been. He rolled off balance and pushed the rifle out before him; he pointed, fired, and the gun kicked him in the side of the face. The warrior went down, staring at him. As the Indian hit the earth, Zeb heard the breath go out of his powerful body. The Comanche hesitated, then lifted his chest from the ground. The boy stared, fascinated, as the man began to crawl toward him. Paralyzed, he watched as the warrior continued to come, halted, reached with thick, powerful fingers, failed, and began to crawl again.

Zeb drew his knife and backed as close as he could against the dugout. He held the blade out before him, cutting edge up, and waited. The brown hand tentatively stretched out again, opening and closing, pincer-fashion, like a crawfish's claw. Just as the boy was about to slice at it, a glazed look came into the Indian's eyes and, with a final, trembling effort, he threw himself at Zeb Cather. His hand clutched and bit at the dirt, shook, and was still—he died staring at the twelve-year-old Texan. The boy looked over the Indian; Billy Cather was standing in the doorway and there were tears in his eyes.

Chapter 11

Everett Randall kicked away the heavy saddle blankets and let the early morning chill and the sounds of impatient horses draw off the effects of sleep. "All right," he said, "I'm coming!" He reached down into the hay and grabbed his boots. Shrugging them on, he yawned and walked quietly across the hayloft to where a pitchfork leaned up against a cobwebbed rafter. Below him, he could hear the expectant stomping of hungry horses. "Hang on down there, it's a-comin'."

In short, quick strokes, he began to pitch the hay from above and it dropped into each stall's feedbin. It always amused him how a horse would go right after the first forkful by shoving its head deep into the bin. The rest of the animal's meal would fall down on its head. That wouldn't happen with a mule–he'd stand back and wait until he got his full share, and then come forward to eat. But any fool knew a mule was smarter than a horse, Everett would think to himself. As he worked his way along the edge of the loft, he began to whistle a song he'd heard from another time.

Since the Easterner had whipped Jeb and Ernie a month earlier, Everett had taken a new outlook on life. The Ratons could be beaten, would be beaten. Something was going to explode here in Running Springs; you could almost feel the tension in the air when one of them rode in. Even Junior Raton had taken to always keeping his back to the wall and did all his drinking at a table up front where he could see the sheriff's office through the grimy window of the Concord Saloon.

On the nights when the Ratons came to town, Zeb Cather walked around the plaza like a puppet being jerked by strings, and kept away from open alleys. Usually the short, solid form of Darby Buckingham strode along beside him. They were a contrast—the one tall, rugged, and every inch a frontier lawman from his sweeping wide-brimmed Stetson to his high-heeled boots; the other a collection of roundness that started at his blunt-toed shoes and carried through the sloping bulges of heavy chest and shoulders. A tree-trunk neck disappeared into a heavy-jowled face, and the whole picture was topped by the round black derby hat.

Yeah, Everett chuckled, they were quite a pair. It was obvious the two men liked each other. Except for breakfast, which Buckingham was forced to share with the widow Beavers, they even ate their meals together. It was only when Sheriff Cather picked his horse up at the livery and rode toward the mountains to circle and watch the Raton spread that they were separated. Everett guessed the Easterner was uneasy around horses.

There were a lot of people in Running Springs besides himself who wondered at the alliance between Cather and Buckingham. It made a strange combination but had at its core a singleness of purpose—the bringing to justice, one way or another, of the Ratons.

Everett had made his decision. He'd stand or fall beside his friends. But against the Raton guns, he knew the odds of winning were damned small. He had bleakly sized it up—an aging lawman who had earned the right to live the rest of his years in peace, and who'd be forced to draw against Junior Raton knowing he couldn't match the man's speed; a polished gentleman from New York who carried dynamite in either fist but probably had never fired a gun; and himself, a man who'd never been anything but a smalltime rancher and who, when trouble came, couldn't be soberly counted on. So there it was, an over-the-hill lawman, a city slicker, and a drunkard. No wonder most folks thought it a losing combination—no wonder the Ratons were sure of it.

He finished pitching the hay, and in the barn's half-light, moved cautiously toward the main doors. He unlatched them, and they swung creakily outward to tell the still yawning town that it was Saturday and business as usual.

The rifle rested darkly against the first stall. Everett Randall regarded it, started to walk by, then gave in to his impulse. He examined the Winchester with a critical eye. After a moment he nodded with approval. It was clean. It gave him a feeling of confidence; perhaps there was a chance. Today maybe—this was Saturday and they'd ride in to town to drink, gamble, and raise hell.

Now was the time, he decided. If he was going to be a help in the showdown, he had to be sure the rifle was close by when the time came. Across the plaza, the Concord Saloon would be opening soon for the few cowboys in town who still had enough drink money to ease the pain of last night's hangover.

Had anyone been paying attention, they wouldn't have thought it particularly unusual to see old Ev, wrapped in a dirty horse blanket, drunkenly lurching toward the saloon at that hour. A man with his kind of need wasn't particular how he looked when he went to beg the morning's first drink. Everett came staggering through the Concord's swinging doors and, once inside, straightened to regard its sole occupant behind the bar.

Carl set a dish towel down and said, "Didn't see you in here last night, Ev. Some of the boys was askin' for you to do a dance or something for drinks. I told them you probably had a bottle somewheres. Look, I'll pour you the usual setup to get you started, then . . . Good gawd a'mighty, Ev! You ain't going to shoot me for a bottle, are you?"

"Hell, no. What's got into you anyway? You been hittin' your own stuff?" Everett growled.

Carl sighed and mumbled a little sheepishly, "No, I just ain't used to seeing folks walk in here first thing in the morning totin' a Winchester under their horse blanket."

Everett laughed. "Forget it. The whole town's riding the raw edge waiting for something to explode."

"Is that why you got the rifle?"

Everett nodded. "I want you to keep it under the bar for me. If shooting starts, jest heave it in my direction and duck out of sight."

"You expecting trouble in here tonight?"

"Maybe. They'll be in town, seeing as how it's Saturday."

The bartender slammed his fist on the wood. "I wish to God they'd stay out of here. Go drink somewheres else. Every time they come in, they bring their crew along and the lot of 'em run off all my regular customers. Except you, Ev," he added, fighting to keep panic out of his voice. "Let's have a drink. Just thinking about them coming in here tonight—Junior sitting over by that window, staring at the sheriff's office . . ."

"No thanks, Carl. I don't need one this morning. But you go ahead."

"You don't need one?" he asked disbelievingly.

"No."

"Then I'll drink yours."

Everett nodded. "I'd like a glass of tea if you have some."

"Tea!"

"Yeah. That's what I'm going to be drinking in here from now until this trouble's over. It's the closest looking thing to whiskey, I reckon. Figure I might as well start trying to get used to it now as later."

After twenty minutes and a lot of fussing, the tea was ready.

"Phew . . ." Everett gasped, spraying the tea across the bar. "It's a good thing I didn't start this stuff earlier; I'd have died of poisoning long ago. Maybe you could pour jest a drop or two of grasshopper juice in there to cut the taste. Just a drop though, Carl; when you toss me that rifle, I want to be able to use it."

Bull Raton lit an after-breakfast cigar and scowled at the dirty kitchen. "This place is a regular pigpen," he said, spitting at a pile of garbage heaped into the corner of the room.

"I wish we still had Ma to keep house," Ernie drawled. "A man gets tired of livin' by his own cookin' and cleanin'."

Junior Raton muttered sarcastically, "What cleaning? You ain't worn clean underwear since last spring when we had that old Mex woman wash for us."

"Wish we could find something better-looking to clean up around here," Ernie said, ignoring the insult–"something maybe like Annie . . ."

"Damn you, boy!" Bull roared, "you ever mention her name again, I'll whip the life out of you!"

Junior Raton watched his filthy, hulking brother recoil in slobbering fear. His father, he noted with disgust, had egg and beef grease in his beard. Junior stepped away from the table; sometimes, he thought, living with his own hog-mannered family was almost unbearable. One of these days he was going to shoot down the sheriff so that everyone would see how good he was. Then he'd get his share of the money, maybe more, and just ride the hell away from all of it. He could do better on his own with a gun. Except for the old man, the others were fools; even the old man, at times like this, was a pig.

"When are you going to let me put a bullet through Zeb Cather? He's taken to watching this place all the time. Our cache of money is damn near gone. With him always hanging around, we ain't been able to work anyone's cattle onto our range or pull a job in months. How in the hell are we going to meet next month's payroll, the damn spring sale money's already gone."

Bull spat angrily. "Damn it, I know we need money. If your

two brothers here would stop drinking so much rotgut at the Concord . . ."

"Aw," Ernie objected, "we don't drink that much, Pa."

"That's right, Pa. We just been going there in the hopes of catching that eastern city slicker when he wasn't with the sheriff."

Ernie snarled, "Yeah, we're fixin' to kill the son of a bitch first chance!"

"Smart, ain't ya?" sneered Bull Raton. "You two get all liquored up, the derby man walks in, and you shoot him. Then, while you're celebrating, in walks the sheriff and puts a bullet in each of your worthless hides. Stupid! That's what you are–stupid. Ain't neither one of you stand a chance against Cather in a gunfight!"

"I would though," Junior said coldly. "Why don't you let me face him, Pa? With him out of the way, Jeb and Ernie could walk right into the Antelope Hotel and shoot the Easterner and nobody would try and stop them."

Bull sat quietly, thinking and smoking. Then he said, "All right, we'll kill the sheriff."

"When?" Junior smiled.

"Tonight, when he's making his usual check around the plaza."

"It's about time, Pa. I've waited for this a long while."

"No, not like that, son. We'll do it my way or not at all. I taught you boys that it's stupid to take chances lessen you have to."

"But, Pa . . ."

"Dammit, Junior, I said it was stupid! You could beat Cather, but he might catch you with a wild bullet on his way down. Or he might roll and put one in you even as he was dying. He's that kind, and it's a chance you don't have to take. Tonight we kill the sheriff. After that, if Jeb and Ernie want to get liquored up and go shoot the city slicker in his bed, it's all right with me. Now, gather around this here table, and I'll show you how we're going to do it!"

Chapter 12

"Captain Cather," the Texas Ranger whispered, "it's past midnight and there's a cloud cover blockin' out the moon."

Zeb was instantly awake and came to his feet reaching down for the saddle and blankets upon which he slept. "Are the others ready?" he asked, trying to pierce the darkness.

"Yeah, they're mounted and waiting."

Minutes later, they moved out across the prairie. Each man rode quietly, easily, like men born in the saddle. They traveled as light and fast as a raiding party of Comanches. The Texas Rangers often relied upon their speed and endurance to run down their enemies. If a man didn't have the horseflesh to go with him, he wasn't even considered eligible to join up. Along with a top horse, each Ranger had a rifle, a Colt, and a Bowie knife for fighting. Generally, they had everything else they needed jammed into a pair of stiff leather saddlebags—a packet of salt, maybe some pinole or parched corn, and extra tobacco. That and plenty of ammunition was as much as a Ranger needed to stay alive and do his job in the rough frontier of Texas in 1839.

As they rode south, Zeb wondered if they'd be able to take the Mexican cattle rustlers by surprise. They had to, he knew; everything depended on it. Even with the newfangled six-shot Paterson Colts his men wore, the eight Rangers were no match for a force of more than forty raiding vaqueros. The Mexicans who rode into Texas and rustled herds knew what they were doing. Even now, down in their own country, they'd still be wary and would put up a tough fight when the time came. Still, he and his men hadn't ridden this far to be faced down by the bad odds. It was something a Ranger accepted when he put on his badge. Yet this was going to be as hard a fight as any of his men had gotten into yet.

With the Rio Grande two days behind, each man rode with a sense of urgency. If trouble hit them by surprise, they were on their own and fair game for the first patrol that caught them. Zeb swore softly to himself, "Damn Mexican army!" If Texans were to win their freedom, if the Alamo were to stand for something . . . "The Alamo," he whispered fervently as though it were a prayer. It had cost Texas her best, and it had cost him his brother, Billy.

Zeb Cather's hand fell to the butt of the Paterson Colt. In just the few months they'd had them, the new gun had saved him some good men; he hoped it would again today. Thinking back over the past months, Zeb realized how good the men he commanded really were. Theirs had been one goddamn uphill battle after another. Always outnumbered, they fought equally well against the Mexicans or the Comanches. It just didn't matter which, Zeb hated them both. The Indians had got his pa nine years before, and Santa Anna and his army had butchered Billy and the others. Now there was just himself and the Rangers, and half of them didn't give a wild hoot if the sun came up tomorrow, as long as they saw it setting on a free Texas.

It was less than an hour before sunrise when they heard the lowing of cattle up ahead. Though the night was still black upon them, each man picked up the sounds and smell of the herd. Zeb reined his horse to a stop.

"As soon as we can see where their camp is, we ride in with those cattle between it and us. I don't want anyone making a sound until we are almost on top of the herd. When I fire, we scatter those cattle six ways to Sunday. They won't know

what's happening until it's too late. I want those longhorns to tear out their picket lines, run off their horses. If we let them get mounted, we're done for. Likely as not, they'll have four or five men riding night herd; try and down them first with your rifles. After we drive into their camp, let the ones go that are running away from us. Them that stand up and fight, put a bullet through their hides. There's one more thing," he added quietly, looking at each man in the beginnings of first light. "Remember the Alamo!"

He swung his horse, touched spurs, and they were running toward the dark forms of the herd. Up ahead he saw a match strike light and he pulled the rifle from beneath his stirrup; that vaquero would be the first to die this day. As they raced across the flat ground, jumping sagebrush, sidestepping rocks and holes, Zeb shot a glance to either side of him, and once again he felt the camaraderie, the breath-taking power of good men joined in a common purpose. Across the bend of each rider's arm, a long rifle poked toward the sky.

Standing up in his stirrups, he snapped his rifle up and fired at the spot where, seconds before, the light had leapt.

The entire herd shook to their feet even before the rifle blast had died. As the Rangers came down upon them, the cattle began to run, to scatter as leaves before the storm. All around him Zeb heard the sounds of rifle fire, and then he was in the herd, spurring forward, fighting to keep his horse up.

Ahead, he could see men grabbing for their rifles, others running for the picket lines. Then his gun was firing and Zeb Cather was doing the thing he seemed destined to do–it was kill or be killed.

Zeb Cather woke with the sun two hours high and shining through the jailhouse bars, slanting its way into his office. It was far past his usual time to arise, but the sheriff felt an unaccustomed reluctance to move. Then he remembered that it was

Saturday and that meant the Ratons coming to town for their weekly buying and drinking spree.

Zeb lay staring blankly upward toward the ceiling. Today could be the showdown; he'd been around men like the Ratons long enough to gauge when they were about to explode, and they were ready. They hadn't been able to rustle cattle or move freely in weeks. He'd seen to that by riding a circle around their spread every few days looking for tracks. Nothing came or went without the sheriff knowing of it, and he could sense Bull Raton's hatred building to a head. The man was ready to blow this country apart; the worst part of it was he had the men and the guns to do it.

Junior Raton, he knew, had been held in check by the old man. But the thin lead line of control that Bull held over him was taut as a strip of drying rawhide, and ready to snap. The sheriff could see the longing to draw in Junior's eyes, the need to prove himself the faster man. And, when Zeb saw the young smoldering-eyed gunfighter, he felt older than his sixty-two years–and he felt the fear of a man who sees himself in the ultimate failure of death.

He willed his body to go flat on the cot and closed his eyes, and as he did, a familiar picture moved across his troubled mind. Junior Raton stood straight and lean-hipped in the empty main street of Running Springs. The man was smiling, even as his right hand blurred down to his gun. Before him, Zeb stood resigned and bent and, like an old man, his hand moved toward his own gun in almost comic slowness. Junior's gun was coming up and the muzzle looked like the black hole of Zeb's own onrushing nothingness. The redhead laughed and waited as the sheriff's talonlike hand clutched at his gun; then Junior's Colt was smoking and Zeb felt himself being swallowed again by the black hole. He was sweating now, big drops were erupting across his body, and still the picture wasn't over. Darby Buckingham lurched into view–his face contorted in rage, his heavy arms outstretched. He moved jerkily forward with all the purpose of his being running from his eyes. Before him, Ernie Raton stood cocking and firing a steady killing stream of bullets into the Easterner's wide vest. When Darby fell, the ground shook, but neither Everett Randall or the sheriff moved to help–they were already nothing.

The vision left him then, left him weak and trembling. Zeb opened his eyes and slowly let the sunlight wash the memory away. He forced himself up. "It won't happen," he mumbled. "Not that way, not to them." He moved to the window. Across the plaza he could see the big open doors of the livery stable and the form of Everett Randall sitting in the sun, working over harness. A white, fluffy cloud floated lazily overhead and its shadow passed across the town. But it was a nice day–too damned nice to last, he thought.

Down the street in the Antelope Hotel, Darby Buckingham was being confronted with the usual morning unpleasantness.

"Yoo-hoo!" came the dreaded sound of the Widow Beavers through his door. "Derby, honey, are you awake and dressed for breakfast, you dear thing you?"

"Go away! I'm still in bed," he growled even as he heard the key entering his door's lock.

She bounced into the room and came to rest beside the bed. "Derby, dear, you must learn to try and arise a little earlier for our breakfast. Remember," she pouted in her best little-girl imitation, "early bird gets the worm!"

"I don't care to get the worm!" he raged.

She ignored his remark. "I'm going downstairs to order our usual breakfast. Hurry," she said, tugging at his covers, "or it will get cold!" She gave up the tug-of-war after a few seconds and smiled with resignation. "You are such a big, strong man, Derby. Bye now. I'll be waiting." The door clicked shut, but the man didn't hear it; he was under his pillow groaning.

An hour later, Darby Buckingham escaped from the Antelope Hotel and, with his usual after-breakfast case of indigestion, moved irritably down the street. Turning in at the shop marked simply "Guns," he made his way past the racks of rifles and came to the rear of the room. A frail, bespectacled man was lost in concentration as he worked over what Darby supposed was part of a gun.

His long, slender fingers deftly manipulated the metal parts, and, as Darby watched, what had been a pile of metal springs and gadgets became a gun, small and unlike the heavy Navy Colt of Sheriff Cather, but a gun all the same.

Five minutes later, the man tightened the last screw in the beautifully polished walnut stock and smiled almost lovingly at the weapon.

"It is a thing of beauty, sir," Darby said with deep admiration.

The pale, slender man suddenly started. His light blue eyes looked bigger than they should behind the thick glasses and were full of surprise. "Have you been waiting long, Mr. Buckingham?"

"No, not very. How do you know my name?"

"The whole town knows about you and what you did to the Ratons. And," he added quietly, "what they will do to you. It's the price one pays for living in a small town that is waiting for all hell to cut loose."

Darby eyed the man, a faint smile creeping into his face. "I wasn't aware that the impending trouble was so obvious."

"Oh really? Well, today is Saturday and the bettors in town are saying you won't see tomorrow's sunshine."

"Do you know why I'm here?" Darby asked.

"Yes, probably to buy a gun. I'm glad you have that much foresight, Mr. Buckingham. Have you also had the foresight to learn how to shoot one?"

"Unfortunately, no. I've never felt the need."

The gunsmith shook his head. "I was afraid of that. It takes practice to become a good shot and you just don't have the time." He picked up the gun. "You said it was a thing of beauty. Actually, it is much more than that. It's a thing of power and balance, but it is not a thing of accuracy. In short, it is a .44-caliber derringer, good for one shot up to about twenty-five yards. I think it is your only chance, Mr. Buckingham."

Darby drew out a cigar. "I'll buy it, sir, along with a few bullets, of course."

"Of course, Mr. Buckingham, of course."

Chapter 13

Zeb Cather stood in his office, looking out toward the plaza. "Here they come," he said quietly, "the whole damn lot of 'em. Bull's riding up front with Junior. Ernie, Jeb, and a half-dozen of their best gunmen are tagging along behind. By the way them jaspers keep gawking up at the balconies and down the alleys, they must think maybe I'll shoot 'em from behind in ambush."

Darby Buckingham smiled. "That, Sheriff, might not be such a bad idea. I'd offer my assistance, but I'd miss anyway."

"Have you ever fired a sawed-off shotgun?"

"I've never fired any gun."

Zeb walked over to a tall wooden rack, passed up several rifles, and chose the shortest weapon. "Double barreled," he said, breaking it open, observing two shells, and snapping it shut. "Here," he added, handing it to his friend; "with this, you don't need to know how to shoot."

Darby scowled. 'How does it work?"

"All you have to do is point her in the general direction and pull the triggers. The gun will do the rest for you."

The sheriff moved back to the window. "They're right across from us now, and the way Junior is craning his neck, he figures to put a kink in it. What do you say we step outside? If they're going to make a move against me today, I'd just as soon see it coming."

"After you, Sheriff," Darby said, gesturing with the shotgun.

They stepped out onto the walk as the Ratons and their men were just starting to pass. "Afternoon, Bull. Are you and all your boys riding in for supplies, or did you have something else in mind?"

Bull swung his horse around, big belly jouncing over his saddle horn. "Afternoon, Sheriff. And you," he snapped, "you must be the derby man."

"Some people in this town seem to refer to me in that manner, but you may call me Mr. Buckingham."

"You son of a . . ." Junior Raton swore.

"No!" Bull shouted. "Leave him be for now, son," he said, looking into the twin shotgun barrels Darby held on him. Then, turning back toward the lawman: "We're just riding in, peaceable-like, to pick up some supplies."

"Good," Zeb nodded, "but I don't see your wagon to load them in."

Bull Raton spat into the dirt. "What we came for today won't need a wagon, Sheriff. Let's ride on, boys; drinks are on me. Nice meeting you, Mr. Buckingham; be seeing you."

Darby held the shotgun and let it follow them until their horses were tied and the ten men had sauntered into the saloon. Bull Raton, he thought, was aptly named, only he had gone to pot. Darby looked down at his own stomach. It didn't stick out much farther forward than his face. Pulling it in a little, he felt glad he wasn't really fat like Bull. When the shooting started, at least there would be one man who made a bigger target than himself.

Bull Raton sat rotating the half-empty bottle of whiskey. "Jeb, Ernie, slow down on the rotgut or you'll sure as hell wind up shooting yourselves by mistake. In a few more hours, it will be dark and we can take care of the sheriff."

"And the derby man too," Ernie snarled. "Most of all, I want to see him beg for his life before I kill him."

"What you do after Cather is dead is your business," Bull said. "Drink your worthless selves to death for all I care; drink until you're crawling around on the floor and slobbering over yourselves like that drunk Randall lying under the table yonder. Me and Junior will handle things, just like we always have, huh, son?"

"Gawdamn it Pa," Jeb swore, "why you always ridin' Ernie and me? We're as good as Junior!"

Bull Raton looked at his two eldest sons and snorted, "No, you ain't. Junior is here to do a man's job tonight. He'll put a bullet in the sheriff, but he'll use his brains doin' it—he'll do as I tell him. And when he's finished with the man's work, you and that stupid, muscle-bound brother of yours can go shoot the city slicker—won't be a man around to stop you."

"Hell, Pa, don't forget that it's me who's gonna send that first bullet into the sheriff from atop the hotel. I'm the one's gonna kill him—not Junior, who'll take all the credit, but me, damn you!"

Bull Raton swung his meaty hand, palm open; when it connected with Jeb's face, it sounded like a shot. "Shut your mouth, boy. You want the whole town to hear?"

"Fer cripesake, Pa," Ernie whined, "there ain't nobody around except us, the bartender, and that drunk ol' Everett. And I think maybe I'll walk over there where he's laying slobbering and try to see how many times I have to kick him before he'll sing a song."

Bull smiled and ignored Jeb, who was shaking in his own silent fury. "Naw, let him lie there spittin' and moanin'. I never did like him, and now I enjoy watching him stretched out there. Besides," he added, "it might do you boys good to see what can happen to a man when he ain't nothing no more cause of swillin' down too much rotgut whiskey. Then all he can do is talk big. Ya understand, Jeb boy?"

But Jeb didn't answer; he was moving toward the bar. "Give me another goddamn bottle, and make it fast or I'll slap the hell out of you, Carl!"

Everett Randall lay between two tables, an almost-dry bottle of the bar's cheapest whiskey in his hand. Alternately, he moaned or sobbed and, once or twice, made a pretense of trying to rise. "Bartender, goddamn you, I wanna nuther bottle. Thisn's jest 'bout empty." Then he'd lift the bottle and let the awful-tasting tea miss his mouth and run off his chin to the floor.

"Look at him, Pa," Ernie giggled. "He missed his fool mouth and now he's licking the floor."

As Bull Raton watched, he felt an unexpected sense of revulsion. He turned his head, but the wild shrieking of Ernie made him angry. Here it was again, he thought. There was something about Ernie that, once in a while, caused his stomach to flip-flop. Despite his size, there was something missing in a man who could laugh on and on at a thing like that. "Shut up, Ernie. You fool, shut up!"

"Aw, Pa, I was jest havin' a little fun. I wasn't gonna kick him, cause you told me not to."

Everett was fighting a powerful urge to vomit. The tea and mud from the floor and the hate wanted to come back up, but he fought it all down. Just a little longer, please, give me the strength, he prayed. From his position on the floor, he could look upward through the window. There was some red in the sky and the light was getting weaker by the minute. Soon Jeb would be moving up onto the rooftop of the Antelope Hotel. His view would be perfect, and Jeb wouldn't miss the sheriff when he lowered his hammer; there was just no way in the world he'd miss.

Everett rolled forward onto his face and crawled to his knees. Slowly, with a great deal of determination, his hands fumbled at his belt, trying to unloop it.

"Not in here you don't!" hollered the bartender as he strode around the tables and came to stand over the glassy-eyed drunk. "Let's go, Ev, I'll give you a lift on out of here. Go crawl back of the alley to do your business!"

Everett went slack as Carl lifted him onto rubbery legs. "Thanks, Carl, jest poin me in the right way, thas all." Then he whispered, "When I come back, be ready with that rifle," as he staggered out into the street.

"Come on, Pa, it's dark enough," Junior said, tight-voiced as the batwings swung behind the departing Everett.

Bull tossed his drink down. "Head for the roof, Jeb. We'll be along directly. As soon as we get Cather out into the street, put a bullet in him. And don't miss!"

A few minutes later, they filed out of the Concord–Bull looking for all the world like a man set on doing things his way. Junior was smiling, and a muscle began to twitch high up near his left eyebrow, giving him a curious, winking appearance. Beside him, Ernie plodded along, weaving slightly. One of the six hired guns they'd brought held a steadying hand on his belt to keep him walking straight.

None of the six were in the same class with any of the Raton brothers. Bull wouldn't have a man on his payroll who could outdraw one of the family; he just didn't figure it made sense. But, nevertheless, each of them was a veteran fighter who'd stick in a tight spot. Tonight, it was their job to back up the play if anyone tried to interfere, although nobody figured to, except the derby man, and he didn't reckon to count much.

Jeb Raton came to rest along the top of the Antelope Hotel. He was breathing hard from his run up the stairs to the second-floor landing. From there, he had simply gone down the hall checking doors until he found one unlocked. He had slipped through the empty room and climbed out the window onto the sill. From there it had been an easy matter to hoist himself up to the roof. But he had snagged his hand on a nail and now, as he lay there panting, the blood from the cut ran into the roof's wooden shingles. He crabbed his way up to the crown and peered over it onto the street before him. "Damn!" he swore happily, "what a shot. Like shootin' fish in a rain barrel." Even using a six-shooter as Bull demanded, he couldn't miss at this distance. Down the street, he could see the Concord Saloon. Much closer to where he lay and almost directly across from him sat the sheriff's office. Jeb unhooked his Colt revolver and laid the big gun's barrel across the backbone of the roof. Then he slowly sighted it back and forth down the main street. At that moment, the heavy figure of Bull Raton emerged into the fading light. Jeb moved the barrel and let it slide to a rest on Bull's dirty shirt. "Ought to shoot him dead, gawdamn him. Always taking up sides with Junior agin' Ernie and me–callin' us stupid all the time, like we was just hired hands instead of family!" Jeb's hand shook in anger. "Ought to kill him!" But even as he considered it along the six-shooter's barrel, Jeb knew he wouldn't do it–he was scared of Bull and scared of Junior, and he knew he couldn't kill them both. Slowly, he forced his sights to leave Bull's chest. Maybe some other time, he told himself, and reached into his coat. A whiskey flask emerged and, heedless of his bleeding hand, Jeb uncorked the bottle and settled back to wait for the sheriff to come out.

As Bull stepped out onto the street with eight men around him, he had to smile. Here it is, he thought, Saturday night and not a soul in view. The streets were empty. A man like Zeb Cather was a fool to try and protect a town of cowards. He began to walk down the center of the street. Right beside, matching him stride for stride, was Junior. Bull pushed away a wanting to reach out and pat Junior on the back and tell his son how proud he was of him. But he couldn't in front of the others–after the fight he'd tell him. The gravel crunched loudly beneath his boots; the town was deserted.

Jeb watched them come. Hell, he thought, there wasn't any reason why he needed to ambush Cather just before the showdown. The man didn't have a chance anyway; he was the same as dead, drawing against Junior. But his gawdamn Junior-lovin' Pa wasn't going to take any chances with his favorite's life. He was going to make sure the sheriff never even got a chance to go for his gun—that's why I'm sittin' up here on this roof, bleedin' and drinkin', Jeb thought. So, after I kill the lawman, Junior is supposed to put a few more bullets into the man with his own Colt. That way, Bull had it figured, nobody could say that it hadn't been a fair fight and that Junior hadn't just beat the man to the draw. In the poor light, no one would be able to see different. With the streets empty, however, it seemed to Jeb that the whole point in his being up there was wasted. He tilted the bottle and, as he did, Bull Raton came to a halt in the quiet, deserted main street of Running Springs.

"Sheriff Cather," Bull hollered, "come out and fight. I can't hold Junior back any more. He aims to show this town who's the best man with a gun once and for all! It's going to be just you and him, Zeb; me and the rest of my men are out of it."

Zeb Cather straightened. "Well, this is it. I guess I don't have to tell you I'm proud to have you stand with me. I sort of thought Ev Randall would . . ." His voice trailed off into silence.

Darby looked at the sheriff; then his eyes fell to the shotgun in his hands. His mind skipped back to his last words with J. Franklin Warner: "Believe me, Mr. Warner, I only intend to write about the western adventure, not participate in it!"

He eased his stubby finger through the trigger guard. "Perhaps the power of this weapon will discourage any of the others from trying to assist Junior."

"That's not likely, I'm afraid. When I make my play, be ready to back me up. If you can remember, I'd say your best chance would be to dive for the ground and start firing."

Darby looked up at the man whose story he'd traveled almost two thousand miles to write. What a shame, he thought, that this might be the last chapter. Absently, he wondered if anyone would ever finish the book if he wasn't able to. He hoped so; Cather deserved that and a lot more. Darby wished he could erase, as a paragraph on a page, what waited outside. But it wasn't possible; someone was going to die in the next few minutes–he prayed it would be Junior Raton.

"Sheriff," he asked, "can you beat him?"

The man had his hand on the door latch. It stopped and Zeb Cather turned to face his friend. "Sure," he said, forcing a tired grin. But his eyes avoided those of Darby Buckingham, and the Easterner felt a sense of doom descend upon him as they stepped outside.

Darby moved an arm's length away from the sheriff, and, as they walked out into the street, his eyes took in the group of men before him. Square in the middle, hat pushed back on his head, ivory gun handle glowing whitely, stood Junior Raton. Beside him, Bull towered up, defiant, spraddle-legged. But it was Ernie who caught Darby's attention. He was weaving ever so slowly; his face was turned toward the writer and his eyes held a killing look. Darby took a deep breath and let it go out slowly; this wasn't going to be just between Junior and the sheriff; Ernie would try and kill him.

"They're fanning out in a line," the sheriff whispered. "If Bull lifts his hand to go for it, hit him with both barrels. No matter what happens to me, Bull has got to die, tonight! With him out of the way, the Raton power over this country is broken."

It was almost totally dark now, and Jeb Raton took another pull on the whiskey bottle and set it carefully beside him. He was smiling broadly at the thought of his father and Junior down below, waiting and waiting for his shot. "Let 'em wait!" he swore. It would do the both of them good to sweat a little. Besides, it galled him to think how Junior would get a reputation as the man who killed Zeb Cather. It wasn't fair, damn him! It would be he, Jeb, who shot the famous lawman down. He hoisted the bottle and let it gurgle; then he carefully eased it into his coat pocket–it was time. Jeb swung the Colt around to bring the sights in on the sheriff. He couldn't wait any longer; they had sweated enough down there, now he was going to have the pleasure of putting a bullet into the great Zeb Cather.

Everett Randall burst through the doors of the Concord Saloon. "Carl," he bellowed, "the rifle!" The bartender ducked under the bar and brought up the weapon fast. Then he threw it straight and hard and, in one quick motion, Everett had it and was running into the street. The Winchester was ready and his eyes were jumping along the top of the hotel. There! his mind cried. It had to be Jeb, the darker spot, small and flat against the vanishing skyline. Up toward the sheriff's office, two Raton gunmen turned at the sound of the running boots and began their play; but Everett didn't see it coming; he was lifting the Winchester toward the sky. The rifle blast rang down the street, jerking every man's hand into a race for his gun—every man, that is, except for Jeb Raton, who flopped forward with the grin still on his face and a large bullet hole in his forehead that cut right under the hat brim and drove up through the back of its crown.

There were only two men whose total concentration was not shattered by the unexpected roar of Everett Randall's Winchester. Zeb Cather leaned forward and let his whole body send power into his right hand as it flashed toward his holster. His eyes shut out everything before him except Junior Raton. But he watched in helplessness as the man's gun came blurring up from nowhere even as Zeb's own fingers slapped his gun butt. As Junior's gun came level, Zeb was just starting to clear leather, and the old lawman knew that, on the best day of his life, he could never have beaten the man who was standing before him. The black hole came up, just as in the dream, and then there was nothing, just the falling and the spilling-out of his own gun as he pointed it toward the men who were dimming before him. When the sheriff hit the street, his finger was still jerking off the shots by reflex, even though Junior continued to fire at him.

Darby whipped the shotgun up. It seemed to take forever. Gunsmoke stung his eyes but he could see Junior emptying his bullets into the sheriff. There was laughter in the young man's face and a hideous delight across his lips. Darby knew then what he would do. Junior had to be first. He was going to blow that smile into tomorrow. He turned the shotgun from Bull Raton and started to pull the triggers.

"No! Not him!" Bull Raton screamed, diving in front of his son. "Not . . ." He didn't finish. The words were swallowed by the roar of Darby's shotgun. In midair, Bull's huge body exploded backward.

Junior Raton saw his father lift almost as if drawn up on a string. Before he could move, Bull smashed into him and they both went down in the street. When they struck, the force whipped Junior's gun around, and instinctively he reached out to break his fall. The ivory-handled Colt flew out of his grasp. Frantically his hand swept from side to side, but it was dark and the gun was gone.

A thinking, deadly man under any circumstances, he pushed his father into the dirt, came to his feet, and ran—without a gun, a man was nothing.

Ernie saw his brother race by, the shotgun blasts still ringing in his ears. Dimly he was aware that everything was all wrong. "Junior, damn you, come back!" he cried, staring after the man. Around him everything seemed to have gone haywire. Bull was dead. Men were running. The smoke was so thick he couldn't see. It was a nightmare! Ernie felt his whole body turn to ice water. He bolted after his kid brother. He was crying and didn't know it. Death seemed to have a hold on his pants leg. He didn't think he'd ever get away.

Down the street, Everett Randall poured shot after shot at the men who were still standing. The Winchester worked itself hot, and it wasn't until everything stopped moving that he finally halted.

The sheriff, he remembered, had fallen. Everett felt tears on his face; it was over, he was the only man left standing on the street of Running Springs. He prayed to Annie that one of those up ahead, motionless in the dirt, would be Ernie. Jeb was dead–he had been the first to die. "Annie," he whispered, "I got 'em both like I promised." Then, he began to walk toward where the sheriff lay.

Chapter 14

In almost total darkness, Darby Buckingham crouched over the sheriff and worked to save his life. He had no idea how many times the man had been shot by Junior–it didn't matter at the moment, for, somehow, Zeb still had a faint pulse.

Around him he could hear the rapid firing of six-guns and, over them all, the steady, powerful booming of a Winchester rifle. His back was hunched over the sheriff, and as he worked, his mind tried to prepare itself for the tearing of a bullet that would end his life. The shadows couldn't save him from that; Ernie wouldn't let it happen. When the bullet came, it would be from him.

Darby wished more than anything in the world that he would have killed the Ratons. There had been no honor in the way they had tried to ambush the sheriff, and the elation that had been in Junior's eyes as he shot holes in Zeb Cather was something he knew he'd never forget. He had seen it from the ground and the only consolation he had was the knowledge that Bull Raton had surely died–if only he hadn't jumped in front of Junior, maybe right now they'd have a chance.

The blood came slickly over his fingers as it welled along a groove near the lawman's hatband. After a quick inspection, Darby was satisfied that the sheriff had been hit three times. Besides the head wound, there was one that sliced across his chest and cut through his arm; but the one that might prove fatal was low in the sheriff's side, just under the man's ribs, and it entered from his back. As the writer ripped his shirt into strips to plug the holes, he swore in a harsh, shaking voice, "Junior Raton, you outdrew him—that act I can understand. But that didn't satisfy you, so you went and shot him in the back when he was on the ground. If by some miracle I shall exist through these next few moments, I swear you will pay for this deed with your life!"

Three quick shots were followed by a final rifle blast—then a heavy stillness fell upon the street. From a distance, the crunch of boots plowed its way into Darby's awareness. He reached into his pocket and brought out the single-shot derringer. The footsteps carried into a patch of light that struggled weakly through somebody's storefront window. As the man's outline passed through, Darby Buckingham lifted the gun, took aim, and fired.

Everett Randall threw himself into the street and jerked the Winchester out before him. There was one left; maybe it was a Raton—Ernie would be hard to kill. He eased the sights toward the spot where the man had fired. His finger was tightening when Dolly Beavers struck a match and put it to the porch lamp of the Antelope Hotel.

The flame reared up within its chimney and jumped across the street with an aggressive surging. The light cast away the darkness where Darby Buckingham and Zeb Cather waited. "Derby, Derby, are you all right?" Dolly cried at them. Then, blinking and stumbling, she raced toward the sheriff's office.

"Get back inside, Mrs. Beavers!" Darby roared. "They're still shooting at us!"

His words went unheeded by the woman; but, in the street, Everett Randall listened, and his trigger finger slowly began to relax. As the woman swept past Everett, he laid his head down and gave thanks that he hadn't killed the last friend he had in the world.

Dolly's cries unlocked the hidden humanity of Running Springs. Lights began to blink through the windows along the main street and finally, they came to a full circle around the plaza. Small groups of people grew in numbers as they moved toward the site of the gun battle.

Darby Buckingham rose to his feet, lifting Zeb Cather's limp body and, with wet, unseeing eyes, he hurried toward the doctor's office. Beside him, Dolly was crying softly, the light from the Antelope Hotel shimmering through the tears. As they passed, Bert and Wes shoved empty six-guns into their holsters. "Well, I reckon we helped pull it off," Bert drawled.

Wes let out a slow sigh of relief. "We done our share, partner–us and old Everett out there. I never did see a man who could handle a rifle like that feller. Let's get a drink; we earned it!"

On a dark back street, Ernie Raton saw a horse. It didn't matter that it wasn't his own, any horse would do as long as it took him away from Running Springs. His hands were shaking and he fumbled, cursing, to get the reins untied; then at last he vaulted into the saddle. The stirrups were far too short and his long legs kinked up high at the knees–but he didn't care. Whipping the animal, he rode bent, doubled-up almost, and as fast as the horse would run. He was more than a half mile clear of the town before he began to think straight. Then he reined toward where he had always gone when he got into trouble, but this time, it was different–Bull wouldn't be there.

The shock of the gunfight held as he shoved the horse toward higher country and their headquarters. The ground ran on, black as ink. Over rocks, through brush, in a nightmarish ride, Ernie Raton somehow felt he would be safe if only he could make it to the ranch. Once there, they'd pull the family together; Bull would . . .

"Pa," he murmured, "what am I gonna do? You and Jeb–nobody left except . . . except . . . Junior."

As he passed onto his own land, he began to think more clearly. Junior would come back to tell him what they had to do. In a way, he thought, he was lucky. Junior had the brains, and he had speed to kill anybody he wanted to. Besides, he reasoned, as the hope began to rise inside him, the sheriff was dead now; there wasn't a person in town that could stop him. He remembered the derby man, and then Everett Randall. He'd bolted, and they'd stood. "Run, damn you!" he yelled, whipping the horse again. As soon as Junior came back, he'd tell him about Everett and then they'd ride back to Running Springs and kill them for what they'd done. "That drunken bastard, should have kicked his head in earlier, should have, should have!" he hollered between clenched teeth.

Junior Raton slid the dripping, chest-heaving horse into the yard. His eyes were dilated and bloodshot. He jumped off the animal in a dead run and crashed through the ranch-house door. A gun! he had to get himself a gun! Then he had to ride. It was over—after tonight he was going to be a wanted man. But a smile curled his lips—he would be famous; he'd outdrawn Sheriff Zeb Cather!

He strode through the main room, past cowhide chairs and over a buffalo-skin rug, then slanted right past the big rock fireplace and shoved open the door to his room. On a rough wooden counter, he fumbled for a match, saw it catch, and touched the lamp. The light cast its flickering glow over the room and revealed an arsenal hung to the walls on horseshoe nails. Guns of every description lined the interior of the room. For a moment, he considered loading his best weapons on a pack horse and taking them with him; but no, as a professional gunman he'd only need the six-gun, and, besides, there wasn't time. He let out a sigh of regret; he'd have to leave them—except for the Remington rolling-block .50. It drove a big, 400-grain bullet. Most people just called it the buffalo gun, and if someone tried to follow him, he could kill them before they even approached a Winchester carbine's range.

Moving to a dresser, he dug under clothes and felt his fingers go around the Colt. When he pulled it out, its white ivory handle gleamed and, with the feel of the gun, his whole body seemed to lift. He held it, looked at it, and after a little while, his breathing slowed to normal. It was the mate of the one that had killed Zeb Cather, the one he'd lost in the darkness of Running Springs.

He strode to a mirror and dropped the weapon lightly into his holster, then looked up at his reflection and smiled. Junior Raton liked what he saw; he looked like a gunfighter–a man who commanded respect and fear. He shifted his feet a few inches farther apart. "Now!" he rasped. Before the word had come full from his throat, the gun was up and pointed at the image of his stomach. He drew twice more, then pushed the Colt firmly into his holster.

Setting his hat at a slight angle, he surveyed himself with satisfaction. He was twenty-two years old, and he would make himself known among men. "Yes, Mr. Raton, it's time you moved on to bigger and better things. There is too much to do for a man of your skills and talents." Nothing could stop him–life and money were for the taking if a man was the fastest. From now on, his gun would take him to the best places.

Junior Raton picked up the buffalo gun and blew out the lamp–he was a happy man. Five minutes later, he was stuffing several hundred dollars worth of greenbacks and three pouches of gold dust into the tops of a pair of saddlebags. "Sorry, Pa," he smiled; "I always knew you was holding out on us–but I reckon you got no need for the likes of this now. Besides," he chuckled, "I know you'd rather I got it than Jeb or Ernie if they'd lived." He was tying down the straps, moving toward the door, when he heard a horse's hooves drum into the yard. Instantly the gun was in his hand and Junior moved silently to take cover behind the couch.

Ernie Raton breathed a sigh of relief when he saw the horse. It had to be Junior; things were going to be all right. He and his brother would settle the score in Running Springs before the night was over. "We'll show 'em," he mumbled, climbing down from the lathered, trembling animal. "Junior," he bellowed at the house, "Junior!"

Behind the couch, Junior Raton swore. "Ernie! Of all the damn luck. How in the hell did he make it?" The thought of the gold came to him. He pulled the hammer back as his brother came through the door.

"Junior! Jeezus, I'm glad to see you made it . . ." He stopped and looked at the Colt pointed at his chest. "Come on, brother, put the gun away." He smiled. "There ain't nobody coming after us. Say, would you like a drink? I'm going to have a stiff one," he said, moving toward a bottle sitting across the room. "I'll pour you one too, then we're going to ride on back there and kill them sons of bitches!"

Junior surveyed the man's back. He's too stupid to kill, he thought disgustedly. How would it look to folks if a famous gunman like myself shot his own dumb brother in the back? "Not good," he sighed, letting the gun drop; "it wouldn't do at all."

"What's that you say?" Ernie asked, pulling the bottle from his mouth. "Here, Junior, take a drink; you're gonna earn it before the night's over."

"Damn you! I already have–I outdrew Zeb Cather tonight; beat him hands down, you overgrown slob!"

Ernie set the bottle down hard. "Ain't right you should talk like that to me. Ain't right at all," he said. "I'll beat the . . ."

The gun came up to its former position on his chest.

"Damn, Junior! I didn't mean it," Ernie said, eyes going wide. "I was just funnin' ya, brother."

The hammer cocked back with an unnaturally loud sound. "I ought to kill you for all the times you whipped me as a kid. You ever call me Junior again, or try and lay your hands on me, I'll blow your dumb head off!"

Two brushes with death in one evening began to overcome Ernie. "Don't kill me. We're of the same blood, all that's left of the family. Please, I'll call you any damn thing you want, but for God's sake, don't shoot!"

"You'll call me . . . J.R. Yeah, I like that. From now on, it's J. R. Raton. That's a name fitting for a gunfighter."

"Sure, J.R. I got it, Jun . . . J.R. I'll remember, honest I will. We'll make 'em pay back in Running Springs, as long as we stick together, we'll . . ."

"Shut up!" Junior roared, sounding for all the world like Bull Raton. "I'm not going back there. Zeb Cather is dead! I beat him and he was the only one in the whole town worth killing."

Ernie blinked, disbelieving. "But what about the derby man, and old Ev? We gotta pay 'em back!"

Junior shoved the Colt into his holster. "If you feel honor bound, then go ahead. I've done what I set out to do. Likely as not, with Pa and Jeb dead, a lot of folks back there will start thinking about things different now. We're cut in half–I don't aim to ride down that street and let someone ambush me with a rifle! I'll tell you something else, stupid. With Zeb Cather dead, those folks are going to send for lawmen, or form a posse and come after us. I can kill any three men in an open fight, but I got too many brains to take on a lynch mob. We're through in these parts; it's been coming for years, but Pa was too stupid to see it." His voice dropped. "Ernie, you go on back to town and settle the score, but I'm leaving before they come here for a rope party!"

Ernie stood in the center of the big room staring at his brother. Running out now was wrong, he knew, wrong as hell, but maybe what Junior said was true and it couldn't be helped. He remembered the outline of Everett Randall, standing down the street firing shots into the men around him, not missing at all. "I guess you're right, J.R.," he whispered. "I need your help in thinkin' things out, that's all. Where are we going?"

Junior slung the pair of heavy saddlebags at his brother. "Here, carry these. We're going west. Maybe toward Nevada and the goldfields."

Chapter 15

Darby Buckingham stood inside the doctor's office and watched the night fade. One room over, Zeb Cather lay swathed in bandages, his breathing shallow and ragged. He hadn't regained consciousness and the doc wasn't sure he ever would. A soft knocking was followed by the lank appearance of Everett Randall squeezing through the door. "How's he doing?"

"Not at all well. He lost a lot of blood. The head wound is more serious than I'd first suspected. The doctor says even if he lives, he may never regain his senses."

Everett shook his head dejectedly. "He was the best man this town had; ain't nobody gonna replace him. The hell of it is that there isn't anyone that even seems anxious to go after Junior and Ernie."

Darby's eyes narrowed. "Do you mean there won't be a posse?"

"That's right. From what I can gather, most folks think that with Bull Raton dead, the power is broken and peace will come back to this range. Could be true, I suppose."

"Yes, but the sheriff was ambushed, shot in the back!" Darby protested.

"I know, but the townsfolk figure to wait for the U. S. marshal to arrive and go after them."

"But the Ratons might escape! By the time a marshal arrives from Cheyenne, they could have disappeared completely."

"They would have. Adios, Derby Man. Take care of the sheriff."

"What do you mean 'would' have?"

"I mean that I'm going to try and stop them. I pledged to Annie I'd get even. Ernie is gonna pay."

Darby nodded. "I can understand your vow. Last night, in front of the sheriff's office, I swore Junior would pay for shooting Zeb in the back. I meant what I said; I'm going out with you."

"And if they've already gone?"

"Then I'll keep going until I find them," Darby said quietly. "There's nothing more I can do in this town. Whether or not the sheriff lives is beyond my power–whether or not Junior does is another matter entirely!"

Everett Randall frowned. The man's mind was made up, he could see that. But Darby couldn't know what he was up against. As for himself, he wasn't thinking past putting a bullet in Ernie. To do so, he'd have to ignore Junior's first shots–but that didn't matter, he had just one thing left to do before he died. "If you come with me, you're probably going to get killed, Mr. Buckingham. I'm going after Ernie; I wouldn't want your death on my conscience."

"It needn't be, because, with or without you, I'm going after Junior."

"Then let's get you a horse and outfit. We'll leave in an hour," Everett said.

Outside, the air felt cool; the freshness of it braced Darby and brought his mind from the fog that had held it inside. He followed Everett down the boardwalk until they came to Dooley's Mercantile.

Inside, they saw the slender storekeeper packing boxes onto already-overladen shelves. "What should I purchase for the trip?" Darby asked.

"You should have a new set of clothes, some boots, a Stetson, and a sheepskin overcoat."

"My clothes are adequate; as for a Stetson–that's out of the question!" Darby said, running a hand over his black hat.

Everett saw the determination and decided arguing would be a waste of breath. "If you ride with me, you'll have to at least wear boots," he insisted. "Otherwise, your shoes will go through the stirrups and you'll wind up being drug to death!"

Darby thoughtfully considered his shoes. An unpleasant mental picture of himself bouncing along upside down across the prairie jolted its way across his mind. "All right, I'll wear boots, but that's the extent of it."

"Fair enough," Everett said, grinning, as a pair were brought out for inspection.

"There," the storekeeper said, admiring the dull gleaming leather. "Stand up and walk around some to get the feel."

Darby cautiously rose, higher and higher, and a smile began to play across his lips.

"Damn!" Everett chuckled. "Now, you're as tall as the next man. Reckon you just been at a disadvantage in these parts!"

Darby tottered unsteadily around the store. His feet seemed to slide into the point toes as they ran down at a sharp angle from the high leather heels. Once, he lurched off balance and seemed in danger of toppling, but quickly he steadied himself against the cracker barrel.

"Nobody said boots were for walkin'." Everett shrugged. "But they sure as hell put some altitude on a man."

After purchasing supplies, they stepped outside. The town was fully into its morning stride and Darby surveyed it from his new five-foot-eleven perspective. "I'll go back to the hotel and gather up a few things, then meet you at the livery. Buy me a horse that's friendly," he said, jamming some money into Everett's hand.

Randall grunted knowingly. "Don't worry, I already got a good one in mind. By the way," he said, smiling, "you're not going to let the widow woman talk you into stayin' are you?"

"Don't be absurd, man!" Darby said, swaying away toward the hotel. As he lurched along, he considered stepping into the alley and entering the Antelope Hotel through the back door. However, he discarded the idea as being beneath his dignity.

At the front door, he paused and tried to peer inside. But the lobby was shadowed, unpenetrable. Taking a deep breath, Darby plowed into the hotel.

"Derby! Oh, Derby, honey," she shrieked, racing across the room and slamming into him. The force of the widow woman rocked him off balance and, on tall heels, he teetered, then crashed over backward. Dolly Beavers came down on top of him, and the weight of her caused Darby's lungs almost to collapse.

"Oh, Derby, I'm sorry! Are you hurt, darling?" she said, fumbling to loosen his tie.

On the third gasp, Darby swore, "Damn boots!"

"Good morning, Mrs. Beavers, Mr. Buckingham!" came a greeting from an older couple emerging from the dining room.

"Oh, good morning to you, Judge Trippet, Mrs. Trippet." Dolly smiled upward at them. "Did you enjoy your breakfast?"

"Yes, very much indeed," the judge answered, smiling.

Darby Buckingham felt the incredible softness of the woman pressing downward upon him. He stopped squirming and gave up the idea of throwing Dolly across the room. The perfume he had always hated was missing this morning; she must have been too upset to remember it. Instead, the sweet scent of the woman filled and found favor within his nostrils. As the Trippets and Dolly conversed on the weather, an upcoming social function, and other trivia, they seemed entirely oblivious to Darby's own awkward and absurd predicament. The ridiculousness of the situation struck Darby and he had to force himself not to laugh. He decided to relax, and surveyed her upturned face. It was a good, handsome one, he realized. It had honesty and character. Perhaps a little too forceful in the jawline, but her hair was soft as it cascaded gracefully around her neck. Darby felt and rejected a strong impulse to lift his head and smell it.

Instead, he relaxed and gazed upward, amazed that he had never noticed the rich color of her hair, or the soft rising and falling way her breasts pushed at their confinement.

"Derby, Derby, you naughty boy," she teasingly interrupted his thoughts, "what are you staring at?"

He felt the color rushing to his face. "Dolly, I must leave Running Springs this morning, so you'll have to let me back to my feet. I will not rest until justice has been done and Junior Raton is held accountable!"

"Derby, please, no! He'll kill you!" she said, trembling over him. "You're a gentleman, strong and brave, but not a gunman."

Darby watched as tears began to well from her eyes. Dimly he was aware of the passage of other diners, but he ignored them. "I must go, Dolly. I don't propose to let myself get killed if it's at all possible to avoid it. Besides," he assured her, "Everett Randall is accompanying me; there isn't a finer rifleman in this country."

Tear after tear swelled, then plunged wetly to his face. "Will you come back to me when it's over, Derby?"

"Of course, Dolly. I'll come back if I can."

Her arms went tight around his neck, and her lips were full, warm, and promising. Lying under her, on the lobby floor of the Antelope Hotel, Darby forgot, for a moment, the killing he intended to do.

Everett Randall was waiting. He was perched on the top rail of the livery's corral and, before him, stomping impatiently, two saddled horses were ready to ride. Under Everett's stirrup leather poked the dull-brown walnut stock of his Winchester—under Darby's the short, double-barreled shotgun's butt protruded meanly.

Still rocking, Darby traversed the street, carrying the few

belongings he felt he must take. Among them, tucked securely between some underwear, was the unfinished manuscript on the life of Sheriff Zeb Cather. He had packed a fresh notebook, pen and ink. Staring over at the doctor's office, he wondered how the story would end.

"Have you ever ridden a horse before?" Everett asked.

"No. Up until now, I've been fortunate in that respect. Is this the animal you've chosen?"

"Yep. He was a little more 'n I'd pay for one of my own, but then you're more of a man to carry."

Darby viewed the horse skeptically. It had a crooked white blaze that struck downward across its forehead and contrasted with the blackness of its coat. Other than the blaze and a stocking on its left foreleg, the animal was as dark as night, and huge. As Darby warily approached, it rolled its eyes sideways to regard him.

"He certainly is tall."

"Yeah, that's because of them long legs of his. Never seen him run, but I bet he moves right smartly. In case we get ambushed, you'd want something under you with speed to get the hell away."

Darby nodded and, with more assurance than he felt, patted the horse's neck. It jumped back spookily.

"It's that derby of yours. He ain't never seen anything like it."

"Well, he better get used to it, Mr. Randall!" Darby said, leaning over almost backward to shove a boot into the stirrup and heaving his bulk upward. The gelding shifted its hooves, braced itself, and peered around at him. "I don't like this any better than you, horse, but we'll have to put up with each other for a while. Now, let's go!"

As they rode out, Darby felt a large sadness in the leaving. The doctor's office stood quiet, shuttered, and he knew Zeb Cather was fighting his loneliest battle. His office was locked, deserted. Even the Concord Saloon looked reluctant to face the day. A few people came out of the stores to watch and shook their heads negatively, hopelessly, as though the two men's fate was already sealed. But there were others who waved and shouted encouragement–one of these was Dolly Beavers. The shine of wetness was on her cheeks as she called, "Good-bye, Derby, honey. Hurry back. I'll be waiting."

Darby Buckingham forced a smile and waved. They rounded the corner and passed out of Running Springs, heading up toward the Tetons and the stronghold of the Ratons.

The big gelding moved easily into a long ground-covering jog that sent Darby smashing downward into the saddle from ever increasing heights. At the end of a mile, he felt as though he had lost a fist fight. "S-st-stop!" he stuttered. "Let's go on foot for a while."

Everett grinned. "All right, but we haven't time to waste. It's still several miles to their ranch."

Darby reluctantly changed his mind and was still riding when they came into sight of the buildings.

"They're gone!" Everett exclaimed.

"How do you know for sure?"

"Junior ain't opened up on us."

They rode past the empty houses, vacant corrals, and pens, then started southwest. "There are the tracks," Everett said, urging his horse into a gallop. "I hope we can catch them before they get clear of this country." Darby, holding onto the saddle horn and bouncing wildly, hoped so too. A bullet would be preferable to being beaten to death astride a horse.

Chapter 16

Four days later, the high-powered blast of a buffalo rifle whip-cracked across the prairie. Its heavy-grained bullet caught Everett Randall's horse in midstride and dropped it cart-wheeling over him. A second shot whined past Darby's face and he left his horse at a dead run. He hit hard and the shock slammed up through his legs and drove him forward into a rolling dive. Shaken, he came to a stop and lurched to his feet, running back toward Everett Randall. Two more shots came close and then he was diving behind the horse for cover. Behind it, pinned solidly, lay its rider, face white and pinched with pain.

"My rifle!" Everett gasped, "can you pull it out?"

Darby bent down low to the ground. The horse was dead. Occasional fluttering spasms rippled across its muscles; under it, he couldn't even see the stock of the Winchester. "It's too far under, Everett."

"Jeezus! If I don't get my leg and that rifle out, they'll be riding in to finish us!"

Darby pushed his hand under the animal and clawed down the stirrup beside Everett's leg. He felt the wooden rifle butt and managed to get the tips of his fingers around it, but it was hopelessly jammed under a thousand pounds of horseflesh. He jerked his arm free, and, in desperation, shoved at the carcass. The horse didn't move–but Everett did and his face went bloodless.

"It's no use; I can't get to the rifle."

A bullet swept by his face again, and it seemed the shots were coming closer now. "I'm going to try and lift the horse," he said.

"Impossible! Go ahead and push it off."

"No, it would ruin your leg and it wouldn't get the rifle free. When I lift, get your leg out of there and grab for the Winchester."

He placed his hands on the only things he could find to grip—the saddle horn and the cantle. He rubbed his knees into the ground trying to dig purchase holes. It was an awkward way to lift anything and he doubted he could even ease enough pressure off the leg to get it free. But the thought of standing up and getting shot wasn't appealing either, so he bent as low as he could and heaved. A bullet thudded into the horse and his knees lost their hold. He slipped backward and the weight came down again.

"Ahh!" Everett gritted, his eyes squeezed tight together.

Darby felt beads of sweat jumping out all over him. It was too heavy to lift from his knees. He drew a deep breath and surged to his feet. "Now!" he yelled, uncoiling upward—straining, digging with his toes and every ounce of muscle in his body. Slowly, as though it was being lifted out of a sleep, the horse rose from the center until only its neck and hindquarters touched the earth.

Beneath it all, Everett gasped in disbelief, then rolled his leg free. The movement sent a pain through him that was almost overpowering, but he fought it off and his clutching hand streaked for the rifle. When he had finally grasped it and pulled it out, Darby and the horse dropped. The rifle came free and Everett flipped it across the saddle, cocking it in one clean motion. He aimed high and fired. They were too far for the Winchester's accuracy. Everett pulled the rifle to his cheek and tried to estimate the trajectory. Maybe, just maybe, he thought. There wasn't any choice. He watched a sudden puff of black smoke, instantly followed by a flat, powerful booming. The heavy bullet passed, singing evilly and very close. Everett raised the Winchester even higher and pulled the trigger again.

Junior Raton saw the carbine's smoke and, instinctively, jerked his horse around. Somewhere near his left shoulder and close enough to hear its whining, the bullet sailed past. Without bothering to warn Ernie, he sank in the spurs and flogged his horse out of range. Two hundred yards later, he pulled to a halt and waited for his brother.

"Damn," he swore, "he almost hit me!"

Ernie was flushed. "We should have just raced in when we had 'em pinned. Now what are we gonna do?"

"We ride, unless you want to go chargin' in on them. Hell, what else can we do? Randall would drop the both of us before we covered half the distance to 'em. Besides," he rationalized, "with only one horse and with the likelihood of some busted bones, neither of 'em figure to follow us. By the time they're able to travel, we'll be out of this country. Come on, Ernie, let's ride!"

"I don't like it; I don't cotton to the idea of letting them off like this. I say let's stay until we finish them. That way we'll be sure they never come up along our backtrail. Besides," he said, "I got a feeling this won't stop them. They'll keep coming."

"Let 'em! Damn it, are you afraid of that old drunk and the derby man?"

"You know I ain't, but it gnaws at me to let 'em live. I mean . . . what about what they did to Pa and Jeb?"

At the mention of Bull, Junior's face went red. "That's over!" he snapped. "Getting ourselves shot ain't going to help Pa or Jeb now. Likely as not, Bull would call us stupid if we was to ride back there and charge Randall as he drew down on us–and he'd be right, that's just what we'd be, stupid and dead. Now come on!"

Ernie's resolve was starting to crumble; you could see it in the way his eyes shifted one way then the other. Knowing he'd won, Junior added, "Besides, even if they should catch up with us someday, it would be in a new town and I could outdraw them both and have witnesses to call it self-defense. Hell-fire," he added, grinning maliciously, "I could even cripple the derby man so's you could pay him back for whippin' you the way he done."

"Damn you, I told ya he caught Jeb and me by surprise!" Ernie choked up as he balled a huge, white-knuckled fist. "If I ever get another chance at it again, I'll kill him with my bare hands!"

Looking at his brother's red, muscle-contorted face, Junior was once again reminded of the man's sheer animal power. "I know you will," he said honestly. "Ain't no man could whip you without using a sneak punch, especially an eastern, derby-wearin' city slicker like that. Now let's ride!"

Across the distance that separated them, Everett Randall let his clammy forehead drop against the dead horse. "Well, they're going on. Probably figure we ain't likely to be any danger with one horse between us." As they disappeared, Everett realized he felt sick. There was burning pain in every breath he took and his chest felt kicked in. Even though his left leg was busted, the throbbing of it was blanked out by the hurting in his chest. He held his breath as long as he could, then let the air out slowly–as he did so, the pain mounted again and he knew he was badly hurt.

Darby looked down and discovered he was holding his derringer. Feeling rather foolish, he shoved it back into his pocket and turned to help Everett. The man's face shocked him. "How seriously are you injured?"

"It's my chest," Everett gasped; "can't breathe good."

"Can you ride?"

The man's face answered the question.

Darby looked around trying to determine his next move. "Maybe I can find some water and get you to cover," he said coming to his feet. "Don't worry, Everett, I'll get us out of this alive." But the old man wasn't listening; he'd passed out.

The quiet, waving grass reached out flatly and the emptiness of it seemed to contradict his promise. Several miles back, a lonely stand of trees was the only thing that broke the pattern.

Standing under the vast rangeland sky, the Easterner knew he'd never felt so alone or inadequate. What to do now? he thought. The Ratons would vanish, maybe never to be found again. But there was no help for it. Everett would have to be taken care of and the nearest town, as far as he knew, was still Running Springs. It might as well have been New York City for all the traveling Everett could withstand. Gingerly Darby began to examine the man's ribs, one by one. He finished with the right side and started on the other. Immediately, as he touched the lowest rib, Everett groaned. With infinite care, Darby touched each bone, counting upward. "Three broken!" he murmured; "maybe one more." He remembered how one of his own ribs had been broken once in the fight ring. The doctor hadn't seemed worried after he'd determined there was no chance of a lung being punctured.

Darby reached down to examine the leg. It took only a moment to determine that it wasn't a clean break. The lower part of the shinbone humped up sharply. He removed the man's boot and rolled up Everett's pants leg to the knee; the leg was swelling fast, the bones had to be set. For almost a minute he knelt over the break, trying to visualize how the fracture would look inside. Though it was not warm, a fine bead of sweat covered Darby's body as he gently slid his hands around the man's knee and ankle. For a moment, he looked up as though to offer a prayer for guidance, then he pulled.

Everett's whole body jerked as though he'd been shot, then fell back moaning deliriously. Darby let his breath out slowly and regarded his handiwork. It was hard to say. The leg seemed straight now. Still, a person couldn't be sure because of the swelling. Maybe there would be loose bone splinters; only time would tell.

It was very quiet as he knelt there, wondering how best to handle their predicament. The day was growing late, and Darby could sense a chill wind beginning to gather from the west. He uncinched the dead horse, and managed to pry off its saddle. The blankets he spread over the ashen-faced man; then he walked to his horse, which stood grazing nearby. Stepping into the stirrup, he started for the distant trees.

Darby came to the spring. Above him, gold and red leaves rattled drily as the wind became stronger. Looking back across the range, his eyes located the flat, still form of the dead horse. Quickly he untied a looped-over blanket and dropped it heavily to the ground; he hoped he had everything he needed. Near the clear, bubbling water, where the young trees branched up thickly, he knelt in the damp soil and began to hack with a large bowie knife he had unwrapped. The tall, straight cottonwood he had chosen was young and thin, only as thick as his wrist perhaps, but its fiber was stringy tough. Overhead the sky drew darker, and, as the knife sliced again and again, Darby's eyes often lifted warily to watch mounting thunderheads gather and pile ever higher.

It was almost twenty minutes before he was able to lay two straight, stiff poles side by side. He recalled researching the travois in one of his stories and it began to materialize in his mind. With a critical eye, he spread the blanket evenly between the poles and began to cut and unbraid short strands from the end of his lariat. Next, he stabbed holes along the blanket's edges and began to tie each side to the poles with the strips of rope. Although the work seemed slow, and the wind had risen to almost a steady buffeting, it was less than an hour until he hesitantly poked the two poles between the stirrups.

"Whoa," he pleaded to the nervous horse, trying his best to sound reassuring. "Just let me tie these two ends to the saddle and we'll be finished."

He lashed the poles, using the notches he'd sliced. The horse was openly scared, and twice he had to dig in his heels to keep it from bolting away. "There!" he exclaimed, leading the animal forward. At the scraping of the poles, the horse panicked. Rearing, it struck out wildly. Darby saw the blow coming but ducked too late, and a steel-shod hoof caught him across the forehead. For a split second, his hands released the reins and the animal jumped away. Darby hurled himself forward to stop it. "Whoa!" he cried, coming down hard into the dirt. As the horse spun away, Darby did the only thing he could do; he grabbed the travois and rolled over onto it; then he hung on for his life as the big, powerful gelding began to run.

It was the roughest going he'd ever experienced. Although the prairie seemed flat at a distance, everywhere small rocks, bushes, mounds, and weeds flew under the poles, bouncing and slamming at him. Lying on his stomach, he tried to see, but it was as if the horse were throwing stones at him, so he pulled himself as high off the ground as possible and his hands locked on the poles in a death grip.

What passed as minutes seemed like hours, but gradually, the horse began to slow. Blowing with great sucking gasps, it trotted for another quarter of a mile. Finally, on shaking, sweat-streaked legs, the black came to a trembling standstill.

From his position, the Easterner could see nothing but the sky and the grass. Very cautiously, he began to push himself upward. He felt drained, lost, desperate. "Easy, horse," he crooned. "No one will hurt you; easy boy."

The animal was incapable of running. Its chest heaved in and out, deep and fast. Darby slowly gathered up the reins and began to follow the pole furrows back. In a land so empty, the lines seemed unreal. Like giant pencil marks, they drove through the grass and raced evenly out of sight.

Before moving Everett, Darby laced the Winchester along the broken leg. He didn't like it, didn't like it at all. But it would have to serve until he got back to the trees and whittled a suitable pair of splints. Everett Randall was very light and Darby lifted him as easily as he would a child. He laid the old man between the poles. It was blowing a roar now, and, increasingly, pelting bullets of rain slapped at his face or drummed hollowly on the crown of his derby hat. He pulled it down tightly and picked up Everett's saddle. Hoisting it high upon his shoulder, he began to walk the horse toward the far-off trees.

It was almost dark when he made his camp, if a man could call it one. But it was the best he could do. The spot was down between two fallen cottonwoods, over which others had long since grown. One tree was half rotted underneath, and the earth had pushed up as though to bury it. Darby tied the black and stepped between them. Kneeling down, he began to dig and tear at the tree's soft, decaying underside. As he worked, he was aware that only an occasional raindrop made its way through the high green lattice of branches above. When he had carved and dug his way under, there was a hole big enough for two large men. In the last fading light, he untied Everett and tucked him neatly against the tree, close to its woody underside. Afterward, he brought in their gear and stacked it beside him.

The wind was screeching now, and brilliant flashes of lightning cut jaggedly across the sky. Rumbling thunder rolled ominously over the land, bullying everything. The big gelding stood, legs apart, eyeballs extended and white-rimmed, as Darby led it closer to the hole he had prepared. Suddenly a crack of lightning arced crookedly downward to flash against a nearby treetop. The horse reared, but this time Darby held on for his life and he twisted the animal's head downward. On a sudden inspiration, he wrapped his arm over its eyes, and the gelding stood quietly shuddering. How long he remained like that, half-supported by the horse, with the storm raging around them he couldn't guess. His arm had long since gone numb and his mind had followed.

It was sometime near dawn when the wind began to diminish very gradually. Darby unlocked his arm and softly talked to the horse in the darkness. His body ached with a relentless throbbing, but his voice was steady, calming to the animal. "We made it," he said quietly, "and the storm is passing. I need you, horse, to carry us out of this mess; it shall be your favor in return for my getting you through this night." He became silent and listened. "The storm is dying; I'm going to tie you up, and if you try to run off, I'll hunt you down and break your fool neck," he crooned gently, with feeling. The horse stood quietly, watching him disappear under the log–it had somehow understood.

Darby placed his hand on Everett's forehead. It felt hot. "Damn," he swore. Quickly he groped around until he found a canteen. He forced the water between Everett's teeth, then placed a cold, wet handkerchief across the man's forehead. Next he located a pair of saddlebags and fumbled around inside them until he drew out what he wanted. Climbing out of the hole, he sat down on the rotting log beside his horse. Then he lit a cigar and waited for the first salmon-colored fingers of sunrise to reach across the land.

Chapter 17

The dawn arrived cold, damp, and so gradually that it was impossible to determine its beginning. Darby Buckingham shifted his weight and ground his cigar in the earth. Rising, he moved back between the two fallen trees and crouched beside Everett.

"Howdy, Derby Man," came a whisper that sounded very weak and tired. "My fever is gone. I been studying that leg you set and I'm grateful. Near as I can tell, I'm going to pull through this, and I've got you to thank." Everett's eyes shuttered. He seemed to draw inward. "Jesus," he breathed. "Here I am and they're getting away. I . . ."

"Never mind about that," Darby interrupted. "We'll hunt them down no matter how long it takes. Where do you think they'll be heading?"

Everett scowled. "Unless I miss my guess, they'll go where there's money and damn little law except the kind a man carries on his hip."

"Where would that be?"

"From the direction they've been traveling, I'd have to say Junior has his mind set on gold-mining country. Most likely somewheres in Nevada. Maybe Austin or Eureka; could be he's even got his sights on Virginia City, although they've probably got a U. S. marshal."

Darby reached for another cigar. "It's a lot of country we're going to search before we're done, I'm afraid."

Everett nodded. "Yep, but maybe not as much as you'd think. Two men like that are going to make ripples at every waterhole they come across. Junior is the kind of fella that's bent on a reputation. We'll hear about them; don't let that worry you none."

Darby smiled. "Good. I just hope he doesn't have the time to murder others before I have a chance at him."

The days dragged by slowly as Everett began to mend. Each morning, Darby rewrapped tight strips of cut blanket around the old man's chest and cinched it up with rope–it seemed to cut the pain. The leg's swelling went down and, as it did, he readjusted the wooden splints.

Every morning, Darby noticed, there were deer tracks leading to the opposite side of the spring. On the fourth day, after some pointers from Everett, Darby watched the sunrise touch the land and knew a hungry satisfaction as he sighted down the long barrel of the Winchester and cleanly killed a five-point buck with his first shot. The nights were getting colder, and at the beginning of each day he found ice along the spring's watery edges. But Everett was healing quickly and would soon be able to ride.

During these weeks Darby often found himself thinking about Zeb Cather and his reason for coming to this land. No matter how things worked out, he knew he was glad he'd come. He no longer thought much about his apartment at 117 Plaza Street; it seemed too unreal, too distant. It was here, he thought, in this hard land, beside this spring helping a man recover, that was important now. That and finding Junior Raton and killing him if he could. Maybe, too, Dolly Beavers was important; at least she seemed to be at times. There was one other thing that mattered–the book he wanted to write about Sheriff Zeb Cather. He hadn't wasted the time he'd known the man. And so, with notes and a memory for detail, he could usually be found settled down between the fallen cottonwoods, working.

"Barry Waco," Captain Zeb Cather murmured to himself as he gazed at the distant outlines of the town, "if you're still down there somewheres, I'm gonna try and take you in. It ain't the way I'd have wanted it; they gave me no choice just as you gave me none when you ran off after the Escobar murder. You owed me a reason."

So saying, Zeb pushed his gaunt buckskin mare down the rocky slope toward Bowtree, Colorado. With each careful step the horse made, Zeb felt himself being drawn into trouble as surely as one man might be pulled to a bottle or another to a faro table.

In the years since Texas had gained her independence and the Rangers had carved their own legend, Barry Waco had left a bigger trail than most men. Zeb had ridden for him during his first years as a recruit. Even then, the man's courage, daring, and abilities as a fighter had already been established. The first time he'd met Waco, he'd been astonished at his youth. He was young enough to have been Zeb's older brother. Had Billy Cather lived through the battle at the Alamo, their ages wouldn't have been much different.

In Barry Waco he saw everything he'd ever wanted to be himself, and a lot he figured he'd never be. So, several years later, it had been a hard shock when they busted Waco from the Texas Rangers. When it happened, young Zeb had been settling trouble in the Panhandle country. By the time he got the news, Barry Waco had left Texas, sworn never to return. The Rangers were clannish, close-mouthed fighting men. Because they protected their own and vowed to uphold their illustrious tradition, Zeb never did find out what his friend had been accused of. No one would talk about it, although he'd caught rumors of a Mexican family and a killing. Zeb racked his memory—yes, Margarita Escobar had been the name of the girl Waco had been sweet on. Her father had owned a big ranch, right over the border, and he had disapproved of Barry. Then he had been murdered and his daughter hadn't been seen again.

Zeb absently reached up and touched the pocket of his leather vest. He felt the paper crinkle; there was no getting away from it, the warrant for arrest wasn't going to disappear—he couldn't wish it away.

It had been almost two years since he'd last seen Waco in action against three suspected stagecoach robbers. Thinking back, it seemed as though it had happened only yesterday. They'd ridden into a jaded Texas trail town and had seen the men's horses tied in front of a saloon.

"Go on around the back way, Zeb," Waco had said. "When you're there, I'll go in the front and get the drop on them. If they make a break, you can be ready to stop them."

He'd started to protest; Barry always took the most dangerous part of everything.

"Go on, Zeb, I'll wait for ya."

When he was only halfway around, gunfire had broken inside and the sound of the shots had pushed through the wall, catching Zeb standing flatfooted in the dust. By the time he'd raced to the rear door and burst in, there was nothing but smoke and a deathly silence over the place.

Barry Waco stood spraddle-legged and his Colt was still smoking. "That one there is Rolly Gannon," he had drawled as he gestured his gun toward one of the dead men. "He had a reputation for being a first-rate gunfighter. Soon as I walked in, he recognized me and went for it. Fortunately, he started his play without lettin' those other two gents in on his secret. If he had, I don't think I could have got 'em!"

The sound of a glass crashed and Zeb had caught movement out of the corner of his eye. Instinctively, he had drawn just as Waco flashed up his own gun. Their shots had almost blended and, behind the bar, an enormous mirror had exploded. "For Christ's sake, don't shoot!" shrilled a voice. "I don't want trouble. I didn't even know them fellers!"

"Then come out, and keep your damn hands above your head," Waco had snapped.

His bald head running with sweat streaks, the man rose, a dirty washrag clutched in one hand.

"Why it's just the bartender!" Zeb had sighed.

But the man hadn't heard him, because his eyes were wide with awe as they took in the form of Barry Waco. "Jeezus, mister!" he breathed, "I never seen the likes of you and I have tended bar in a lot of towns; poured drinks for some of the best gunmen in the country, but you beat all!"

Waco had blushed and smiled. "Aw, hell, wasn't that big a thing."

"Don't you believe it," the bartender had protested, turning to convince Zeb. "Your friend here just outdrew three of the best gunfighters in these parts. Rolly Gannon was good, damn good, but he got beat bad! If I hadn't seen it personal, I'd never have believed it!"

Waco had turned away, a tinge of embarrassment in his voice. "You made a helluva good draw just now yourself, Zeb. Wasn't but an eyelash behind mine. If either one of Rolly's pards had been as fast as you, why I'd be a dead man."

It had been Zeb's turn to blush and, even now, after all this time, the compliment still warmed him. But an eyelash slower wouldn't get any praises today; if Waco refused to ride back, it would only earn him a pine box and a piece of Colorado boothill.

As he rode forward, his stomach began to tighten and he felt the chill of the wind more than he should. Remembering the ex–Texas Ranger, Zeb knew he wouldn't come back willingly. Maybe down in Texas they'd known that too, and that's why they'd sent Zeb and his gun—the fastest they had. The Ranger drew his coat closer about himself and switched the reins to his left hand. His right went deep into his pocket for the warmth. It wouldn't do to ride in with a stiff gun hand. He wondered how much Waco had changed in two years. Once, they'd almost been brothers. But, as with all things, even friendships die with the passing of enough time. He knew the stories they told these days about Barry Waco, how he'd become a hired gun—a man you sought out when no one but the very best was good enough.

Zeb rounded the edge of town and started down the main street. His eyes swept over the unpainted, rickety board shops and walkways that made Bowtree, Colorado, look like a hundred other frontier towns. Zeb decided that it didn't matter if a town like Bowtree were in Texas, New Mexico, or anywhere west of the Mississippi—it always looked the same, as if the entire frontier had hired one unimaginative master town builder.

Down the street, looking just as he'd expected, leaned the High Stakes Saloon. That was the place where he'd been told Barry Waco conducted business; it was where the fate of dead men had been sealed. Zeb Cather reined and sat peering from his horse, trying to penetrate the saloon's darkness. How am I going to make him come back? he wondered. Why does it have to be me? But even as he asked, he knew. He stood the best chance. Knowing that, he could never have let a slower Ranger do this job; the man's failure and death would have been on his conscience.

He stepped down from the horse and was glad his legs felt steady and strong, despite the uneasiness in his stomach. Then, not wishing to think on it any longer, he pulled his hat down as low as he could and sauntered through the swinging doors. It was a moment before his eyes pierced the gloom enough to take in the quiet poker game that was going on at the back. His heart flopped over like a beached fish as Barry Waco glanced up through the smoke, passed over him, and returned to the hand he was playing.

"Whiskey," Zeb ordered softly.

He paid the bartender and quietly sipped his drink, nursing it until his vision became comfortable in the dimness. Then he slowly pushed his hat back and turned to regard the game. How long before Barry Waco's eyes were dragged up by his own, he didn't know. But with his face exposed, he saw the man start in recognition.

"Well, I'll be damned," Waco said in a tone that carried noncommittally flat across the space between them. "Zeb Cather, my old Texas Ranger compadre. What brings you this far from home, boy?"

"I got orders to take you down to Texas, Waco. I'm carrying a warrant for your arrest," he said.

"After all this time?"

"They got some new evidence and dug up a witness; they figure you're guilty."

"What's the charge, Zeb?"

"I don't know, but I reckon you do. All I know is that it has something to do with that Mexican family that was wiped out just before you left," Zeb offered.

"Do you think I killed the Escobars?"

Zeb drew a deep breath. "It don't matter what I think and you know it. Like the others, though, I'd be interested in finding out what happened to the girl."

Barry Waco pushed up from the table and stepped back. "Seems to me," he said, "you've been jumpin' to some pretty wild conclusions. Thought I taught you better than to take another man's word for the way a thing could have happened."

Zeb let his hands drop to his sides. "I wanted to hear you tell it, but you rode out without an explanation. After all this time, I'm still waiting."

Waco smiled, "They're lying to you. I was better than any man they had and they knew it. I reckon it bothered some of them boys at headquarters real bad, cause they framed me. Who knows, as much as some of 'em hated the Mex, maybe they rode out and killed the old man and his woman."

"They never found the girl; what happened to her?"

"How the hell do I know?"

"Why don't you ride back and we can find out?" Zeb asked. "Look, if what you say is true, I'll stand behind you all the way."

"You'd do that, wouldn't you? Same ol' Ranger Cather," he said, smiling. "Sorry, Zeb, it's over. Get on your horse and ride out of Bowtree. I'll let you go for old times sake."

"I can't do that and you know it," Zeb said, feeling his stomach knot. "I got to take you back, or . . ."

"Die trying!" Waco snarled as his hand streaked down for his six-shooter.

Zeb Cather threw himself at the floor, clawing for his gun. Even before he landed, it came level and began to buck. A heart-skip later, the sounds of it were joined with the booming of Barry Waco's gun. Two bullets plowed into a table beside the Ranger and then he saw Waco begin to crumple on his feet. Zeb's finger kept pounding the slugs into him even as the gunman was still spraying his own bullets across the room. Waco's last shot buried itself in the floor just before his body came down to muffle the sound of it.

The sudden silence was a strong thing, and it held everyone trancelike. Slowly, Zeb Cather rose to his feet and walked around behind the faro table where the man lay. He was as dead as yesterday's friendship. Zeb reached up and yanked out the crumpled warrant. He dropped it to Waco's chest. Then he reached into his jeans and dragged out a gold piece. "Bury him good," he said to the room. He moved out of the saloon and stood on the rotting boardwalk. Suddenly it came to him that Bowtree was the ugliest damn town he'd ever been in. His first impression had been wrong–all towns didn't look the same.

Chapter 18

The Ratons galloped out of the vast, hazy gray stretches of sage to pass around towering Copper Mountain. It rose almost fifty-five hundred feet out of the flat, high desert country of northern Nevada and was as barren as the land that seemed to be trying to expel it. Their backs to the north, they were being pushed by a cold, biting wind that drove them until they finally reached the head of Seventy-six Mile Canyon. It ran out straight, and between its hard, rocky walls, like a colony of busy prairie dogs, thousands of miners worked. Everywhere, their pitiful claims were identified by small mounds beside hard-dug open pits, and the striking of their steel picks blended into ten thousand bouncing echos. These sounds lost themselves in thick clouds of dust, and together they rolled down to envelop the gold-booming town that was Mardis, Nevada.

They sat their horses and stared at the caldron of activity that teemed below them. Born of grass and cattle, they had never seen anything to compare to this—their first sight of a fever-pitched mining town.

There was a long, narrow trail that somehow held two steady streams of wagons and men that moved in and out of Mardis. Huge, creaking ore wagons, brakes screeching, jerked their weight downward and were passed in turn by the driving, cracking freighters moving upward toward the diggings.

Junior Raton punched the spurs to his horse. "Come on," he said; "we wanted a gold-mine town; we found it!"

They located a path and rode down until they came to line behind an emptied freight wagon; the canyon walls were already beginning to pinch inward, so they settled into the procession and, as they passed out of the diggings they were almost immediately followed by a big, hard-braking ore wagon. The grade was steep and the wood blocks smoked. It made them both ride tight-wound. Ernie sat with body twisted and his head constantly snapping backward. He knew that the mules behind him would surely slip and tons of ore come cannonading over them. Once, a mule did step off the trail and almost went down, but the hard-bitten driver who rode above them yelled and swung a whistling whip that like to have stopped Ernie's heart from beating. "Don't worry, cowboy," he yelled through the echoes; "if she breaks loose, you'll be the first to know!"

Ernie swore until his throat went dry and he began to cough, but the driver just laughed and eased up on the brake in quick, grabbing motions that shoved the wagon's team practically over the top of 'em. Ernie's face went blue and his massive fist covered the grip of his six-gun. "Jeezus, I'll kill him, I swear . . ."

"Don't be stupid! Do you want us dead for sure? Ground into the rock by these damn wagons? Put it away!" Junior ordered. But as the sounds of the wagon loomed up behind him, he knew he'd be damn glad to reach the bottom himself. How much farther? he wondered, pulling his horse out of line until his stirrup brushed the rocky walls. He caught a glimpse and swerved back into the center of the line–halfway, they were only halfway–it was like a trip down to hell.

It seemed like a lifetime before they felt the floor of the canyon level out; in reality, it had been less than a mile. The walls quickly began to fan and it became evident to both men that every available inch of ground off the trail was someone's mining claim. The countryside was staked and dotted with shacks, tents, brush-covered lean-tos, and, in the meanest cases, just blankets stretched over the open pits. Junior shook his head in a disbelieving mixture of pity and disgust–they were living like animals.

Beside him, Ernie was thinking about other things, and as they came onto the outskirts of Mardis, his eyes anxiously began to read the signs tacked across the fronts of the buildings. He was dry, so dry his lips felt like boot leather and his tongue seemed two sizes larger than it should have. He'd forgotten the wagon behind him–all he wanted was to get a drink.

Junior watched his brother gawking at the signs, lips moving, as he slowly tried to read one of the few words he knew–saloon. Junior guessed what was on his brother's mind, but he had bigger plans than a bottle of rotgut. He couldn't help but feel angry.

The largest building in Mardis was the towering, two-storied High Stakes Saloon. In contrast to the drab, wind-warped establishments around it, this saloon stood under a fresh coat of dazzling red paint. A huge white-lettered sign hung from its second-floor balcony, telling anyone who could read that Abe Shipler's High Stakes served good whiskey and ran an honest game.

Ernie swung out of the path of wagons and forked his horse in between several others at the hitching rail. Two quick wraps and he was heading toward the open doorway.

Junior shoved his animal in next to Ernie's. He had decided the first thing to do was to get a room and clean up. From the moment people here saw him, he wanted them to realize he was a man to be reckoned with and not just a worn-down, saddle-weary drifter with dust in his mouth. But there was no help for that now; Ernie had disappeared into the saloon, so he flung the reins around the rail and stepped up on the walk. "Damn," he swore to himself, then took his hat off and started slapping at his clothes. The dust rose in clouds, and the more he swatted at it, the more it seemed to come. It was thick about him and it made his eyes water, and it made him mad. He felt his face; there was three days' stubble. A fine figure I cut for being the fastest gun alive, he thought mockingly. Christ! how the hell would anyone know it to look at him? He crammed his hat down low and marched in, almost hoping someone would give him a chance to show who he really was.

"Hey," Ernie yelled from the far end of the bar. Junior Raton felt the gazes of men turning to regard him. He ignored them and irritably strode through the saloon toward his brother, who was waving him on with an already half-empty bottle of whiskey.

In the far corner of the High Stakes, young Ory Riley placed his nearly untouched glass of beer down onto the table and watched Junior as he swaggered across the room. He noted the dust and mentally calculated that they likely had just ridden down the canyon from the north. Even in the dimness and through the perpetually drifting cigar smoke, the tied-down pearl-handled Colt shone cleanly. Ory Riley's eyes traveled over the man, but they centered on his face mostly. He wore a stubbled beard that failed to hide an arrogant, finely chiseled jawline. The eyebrows were laced downward, and as he brushed past miners there was an open aggressiveness about him. Ory smiled grimly; another gunman to add to Abe Shipler's growing stable. Maybe a cut above most of them he decided, noting how his gun hand never pulled more than a short distance from his holster.

Ory picked up his drink and turned his attention to Ernie. Brothers, he thought immediately. But, except for the same blood-red hair and facial features, they were entirely different. He watched as the bigger one upended the bottle with a right arm as large as the calf of most men's legs. With his head tilted back, he drank in great whooping gulps that sent his egg-sized Adam's apple bobbing up and down his tree-trunk neck. A brawler, unless I miss my guess, he decided.

Junior was watching Ernie too. Whiskey sloshed out of the corners of his mouth and wetted the front of his shirt. "Give me that damn bottle!" he ordered, snatching it out of his brother's hands and causing some to spill into and burn his eyes.

The whiskey stung and Ernie yelled, bringing his hands up to cover his eyes. He palmed them hard, and finally, when the stinging was gone, he dropped them and his face was mean as he looked, wet and bloodshot, at Junior. He wanted to hit him for that, for taking the whiskey away in front of strangers. Ashamed, Ernie glanced around; no one was paying any attention, no one had seen it. His eyes stopped on Ory Riley, who sat watching intently. No one but him, he thought, staring hard at the man.

Ory took the challenge, and he locked in and stared openly at Ernie's small, red eyes that were burning with hate and the brightness of chugalug whiskey. Look away, Ory told himself; the man's not to be fooled with. But he couldn't; he had never been able to back down, so he just sat there and stared, waiting to see what would happen.

"Take it easy on this stuff, damn you!" Junior hissed, shoving the bottle hard back into Ernie's chest.

The man turned. "Don't push me, J.R. We got to stick together. Specially," he announced, "in this town which is full of insolent staring son-of-a-bitch miners and ore-wagon drivers!" His words ended almost in a shout and he took another pull, all the while staring over Junior's shoulder at Ory Riley.

Three men beside Ernie swung around at the words. Though none of them were big, they bore the work-hard hands and weather-burnt faces of men who took no truck. "What did you call miners?" the one in the middle asked. Ernie's gaze left Ory and came down to regard the man.

"I said they was son-a-bitches."

The man in the center shifted his feet and then caught a huge fist between the eyes that hurled him bullet-flat past Riley's table. Ory didn't watch him land for he waited to see what would happen next. He didn't have to wait but an instant. A second miner plowed in, swinging for all he was worth. Ernie caught a punch over the ear, then grabbed the man's forearm and broke it over the bar's edge. When the miner screamed, Ory felt his stomach turn to rock and he came out of his seat. He watched as the big stranger reached forward and grabbed the last miner before the man could get away. His hand went around his neck and he lifted him white-faced and kicking off the floor.

"You look like the kind of man should be taught to mind his own business," he snarled over at Ory Riley. "A kid like you has got to be taught better'n to stare at a man when he's drinkin'." Then, one handed, he spun the miner barreling into Riley's table.

Before the man went down, Ory reached out and caught him by the shoulders and pulled him to a dazed standstill. "Are you all right, Pete?" he asked, picking up his chair and sitting the strangled, gasping man down. Pete was swallowing hard, trying to get air, to speak. Ory turned to regard Ernie Raton. "All three of those were good men; they worked for me and now they're bad hurt, mister."

Ernie picked up his bottle and smiled. This was going to be more fun then he'd thought; the kid wasn't going to run out on him.

Ory Riley balled his fists and moved toward the bar. Had anyone needed to ask, he'd have said he was probably fixin' to get whipped bad. He'd also have told 'em it didn't much matter to him, as long as he got in a few good licks of his own. But that was the way Ory Riley looked at things; and that was why, at the age of just nineteen; he'd worn down and licked every man who'd challenged him. It had taken him ten months and a twice-busted nose, but he was the youngest mine manager in the lode and his men worked hard for him. Ory figured it was part of his job to try and settle the score with the big man-buster waiting on him.

He came in, looking much shorter than his thick-shouldered five feet eleven inches. Maybe it was his short legs, maybe just that he never quite came at a man straight up. Whatever, Ory had a way of stepping up to a fight that pulled a person into thinking he was small. But beneath a too-big rough-spun work shirt was about two hundred pounds of muscle, set on moving just one way—forward.

Ernie Raton smiled in anticipation—he had a feeling he was going to have some fun; maybe he'd play with the kid at first to stretch things out. Ernie wiped his hands on his shirt and lifted them. That's when Ory hit him in the face so hard he went spinning over the bar and crashed into a back shelf full of whiskey bottles.

Junior Raton went slack-jawed, shock going all through his handsome, stubbled face.

When Ory spun around to face him, Junior saw they were about the same age, only he was a lot better looking than the miner. It figures, a man didn't learn to hit like that without taking some punishment of his own.

"You want to join in and help him?" Ory asked, mockingly. "After all, he looks to be your own brother."

Junior Raton wanted to fight; he clenched his fists until the knuckles stuck out white, and bloodless, but he couldn't make his feet move forward. It would be stupid! came the thought to his mind. I'm the fastest gunman alive, not a brawler, a man who gets his hands and face broken up. He backed up a step and forced his hands open. "Not like that," he said quietly. "If you was wearin' a gun . . ."

"I don't need one!"

"You're going to need something," Junior said, "cause Ernie ain't done with you by a long shot."

Ory turned to see him coming over the bar—big, mean, and not looking ready to quit at all.

Ernie knew his upper lip was split open almost to the base of his nose. The whole front of his mouth felt numb, and half-way over the bar, he felt dizzy. He saw a bottle of whiskey off to his side and grabbed it. When he drank, the liquor hurt where he was cut, but it cleared his head and he felt the warmth of it steady him.

Ory Riley knew he had shaken the man and it had given him the advantage. Not wanting to lose it, he stepped in at Ernie with every intention of grabbing his leg and heaving him over backward. Maybe, Ory thought, this time he'll land on his head and break his neck.

"Leave him be!" Junior snapped, drawing his gun in a sweeping, fluid motion. "Ernie, damn you, man, get up and fight or so help me I'll turn this gun on you!"

Stretched out full across the bar, Ernie Raton felt that if he could just have one more drink, his mouth would stop hurting and his head would clear. He knew Ory was being held back by the gun in Junior's hand. One more drink, Ernie thought. As he shakily lifted the bottle, he saw Ory standing confident and spraddle-legged, just waiting. "Damn you, boy!" he cried out, and instead of taking the drink he snapped the bottle up and hurled it at Ory's head. It caught him square in the center of the forehead and he went over backward.

"Get him, brother, get him!" Junior urged.

Ernie rolled off the bar and came in with his fists hanging low and ready. He waited until Ory rolled over, eyes glazed, then he hit him with a knee-level uppercut that flattened him.

Ory Riley knew he was beaten. He fought to clear a haze, but felt as if he were looking out the far end of a mine shaft. Ernie was coming in at him, he could sense rather than see it; but he might as well have been trying to lift Copper Mountain for all the good of it. He felt the floor shake under his hands, and braced himself for what he hoped would be a clean, obliviating blow.

Three shots swept across the interior of the High Stakes Saloon. They were loud and blasted tight-spaced into almost a oneness. They were dead accurate too, and Ory Riley felt a hard jarring as the unmistakable impact of two bodies dropped nearby. He willed his eyes to open and let them focus on the lifeless miners stretched out before him. It seemed unreal, but both wore looks of disbelief, and both held guns in their hands.

Junior Raton stood anxious with the familiar smell of gunpowder around him. No one moved under his gun as it slowly waved back and forth. The tension hung, and Junior knew, when the shock wore off, they'd rush him. A man could sense it, and Junior had the sickening feeling that he'd stumbled into something that had been building for a long time–something so big it was going to blow up and take him with it. They'd rush him, knowing he had only two, maybe three, bullets left. And when they did, he knew, there wouldn't be enough left of him and Ernie to hang when they finished. He watched as Ernie backed up toward him and wondered why he hadn't shot him back in Wyoming. But even more, he wondered why he'd just saved his life and wrote out his own death warrant. Stupid, that's what he was, just plain stupid!

Ory somehow lifted to his feet and his eyes focused in on the dead men. "What happened?" he said thickly, breaking the spell.

The response burst out with a concentrated fury: "He shot 'em!" the roomful yelled and surged forward.

"No! It was self-defense!" Junior screamed, snatching Ernie's still-holstered gun and waving it at the mob. "If anyone makes a move . . . I'll drop him."

Ory looked down at the two dead men, then over to the bar; his eyes burned at Junior and Ernie. He'll take at least four or five more good men before we get him, he calculated, and I'll be the first. Jeezus, he thought sickeningly, why didn't those two just let me get beaten and stay out of it. Ory took a deep breath. Maybe if he went low and drove in hard, maybe the gunman would panic and miss. His eyes moved back to the guns in each of Junior's hands as they continued to cover the room. Miss, hell! who are you kiddin'? He didn't miss them two and he wouldn't miss me. Ory straightened up; there had to be a better way. All he wanted was just a hint of a chance.

"Well," he said, "had to use it, didn't you? But it's going to cost you plenty to prove how fast you are."

"What the hell are you talking about? I said it was self-defense. Those two friends of yours would have shot my brother if I hadn't stepped in!"

"Maybe," Ory said, "but as good as you are, you could have winged 'em—or just buffaloed 'em maybe, but instead, you just killed 'em!"

"I had no choice!" Junior said, trying to fight off a sense of disaster that was moving in on them.

"Let's hang 'em!" someone yelled from the rear of the crowd that seemed to have swelled to bursting in the suddenly airless saloon.

"We're tired of honest men being shot down by gunmen," shouted a burly miner through a bear-rug beard. "Hang 'em, I say!"

"What are we gonna do, J.R.? I don't want to hang," Ernie whimpered; "what are we gonna do?"

"Take as many with us as I can. Starting with him!" he hissed, swinging his gun on Ory Riley's chest.

"Hold it! Anybody starts shootin' up my place is a dead man."

Junior Raton looked upward and saw a shotgun with two barrels that looked as big as Ernie's boot tops. Behind it, stood a lean, palefaced man with a black, drooping mustache and a long, thin goatee that hung down over the whitest dress shirt Junior had ever seen. He stood on a balcony that traversed the entire back wall of the saloon. Along its length a half-dozen doors hung open, and, evenly spaced before each, riflemen held steady, leveled shotguns on them all. If they fire, Junior thought, they're gonna have to scrape me along with the rest of this crowd off the walls. But it was a bad thought, so he focused in on the man he guessed was Abe Shipler, owner of the High Stakes. He was so commanding, so immaculately dressed, that Junior momentarily forgot the crowd before him. That's the way I want to dress, he thought, mentally putting himself into the clean, white, starched shirt, the black coat. And I'd look better'n him. See the way the coat's wider at the top than the bottom; makes his shoulders look big when they ain't; good gawd, wouldn't I be a sight in a suit like that! By damned, I'm gonna have me one; I deserve it! Impulsively, Junior glanced at his own clothes, then wished he hadn't—he felt dirtier than he'd ever remembered.

"I happened to see the shooting myself," the saloonman behind the shotgun told the crowd. "Like the stranger tried to explain, it was a clean case of self-defense." He continued slowly, letting his every word drop heavy upon them. When his eyes came to rest on him, Junior felt he had met almost an equal. He had a feeling he'd experienced only once before—the first time he'd witnessed Zeb Cather in a gunfight. Standing there, dirty, unkempt, and staring up at Abe Shipler, Junior wanted to tell him that he didn't like looking the way he did; he didn't like having a brother like the one that stood shaking beside him. But, even more than all those things, Junior Raton wanted to shout up and tell the man that he was the fastest gunman alive and, to prove it, he had outdrawn Zeb Cather—something no man, no matter how fast, had ever done before.

"What's it gonna be down there? I say it was self-defense, same as them two do. Who's gonna be the first to call me a liar and get blown apart?"

Ory Riley swallowed hard. "You ain't going to pull it off this time, Abe. It was murder. You're not the law in this town."

"Nor are you, Ory! I run an honest house here and what I say goes." His voice dropped. "I say those two men are innocent."

"Since when have you taken to standing up for anything unless it's got something in it for you, Abe?"

The shotgun centered on his chest. "Don't push your luck, Ory; you've used up more than your share today already."

"Maybe you're right, Abe," he said, looking around and knowing that he and the rest of the mining men were beaten.

There was no protest on their faces; they knew it too. "Abe, one of these days we're gonna get some law in this town, if we have to do it ourselves."

"One of these days, Ory, I'm going to kill you if you keep pushing me hard enough."

Ory Riley stared down at the two dead men, then over at Junior Raton. Very softly he told him, "One of these days, me and the boys are going to form a vigilante committee and we're gonna hang the whole damn lot of you!"

Junior Raton didn't watch Ory Riley turn and stomp out of the High Stakes. He didn't even pay much attention to the rest of the grumbling, swearing crowd as they picked up the dead men and left. He couldn't tear his eyes from Abe Shipler.

"I never seen a better bit of gunplay, mister. Why don't you get cleaned up and you and your brother come on up for a drink; maybe we could use each other." Then, watching Ory Riley and the miners file out: "There's a job to do–something I should have done long before now!"

Chapter 19

Darby Buckingham stared hypnotized at the lazy, floating snowflakes as they fell sizzling into his campfire. He was waiting for dawn, and the time for leaving. The snow reminded him of his home in New York City and how it made things clean and very quiet. Darby pushed the memory off and peered down at his coffee. It was hot and, as he drank, its steam rose and wetted his thick, black mustache. The moisture ran down the corners of his mouth and disappeared into his new beard.

The wait had not been easy, especially in the beginning. Once the wildlife had become aware of the presence of man, he'd had to range farther for meat, and sometimes he'd failed. Absently, he pulled at the overlapping waistline of his trousers. Nothing fit any more and he knew his clothes hung about him, tight only in the arms and shoulders.

"It's time to get up," he said, walking over to prod Everett Randall gently. A grunt sent him back to the coffeepot.

There was a faint streaking to the east that wouldn't be obscured even through the snow. It was time to leave; yet somehow he almost hated to depart from this place. He had faced a test here, and the fact that they were still alive was evidence of his success. He had known he was more than capable of making his way among men in the cities; but here, it was a very different sort of life struggle.

When he hadn't been hunting or mending, he had worked

on the book about Zeb Cather. With the ax, he'd even fashioned a rough desk. The writing flowed and he had finished late last night–finished, that is, all except the final chapter. That was why they had to leave, and God only knew how it would end.

"Ev, I'm wondering how this is going to come out. I've got to get Junior Raton."

"You will, Derby Man. You wouldn't have been able to a month ago, but I'd give you a chance now." He eyed his friend keenly. "Never seen a man change the likes of you. When you see Junior Raton, he'll think you're a stranger. You're twenty pounds leaner and you look meaner than a prodded polecat."

Darby threw out his coffee and grounds. "We'd better be riding."

Everett wasn't listening. "Just remember what I said. When you see him, don't give Junior time to draw. Before he savvies who he's facing–blow a hole through him big enough to shove that coffeepot!"

Darby thought about the last chapter and the way it had to be written. "Let's get it over with," he said.

"Is the horse saddled and ready?"

Darby nodded. "I packed everything, but maybe you'd like to make sure I didn't tie it on wrong."

"Ain't necessary. Only thing worries me this morning is this snow and the way you keep staring at that fire. Have you changed your mind about killin' Junior?"

"No, and you know better than to ask."

"Yep, damn it, I'm sorry." He looked evenly at Darby. "You know," he began, "it ain't easy to say this, but I never had a man that stuck by me the way you did here."

"Oh now, wait . . ."

"No, let me finish," Everett insisted. "When my Annie was murdered, well, it just sort of took the sunlight out of my life. What you've done for me means a lot. Now, I want just one thing before I go down, and you know what that is. I guess it's wrong for a man to change like I have. Annie would say it was agin' the Good Book. But damn it! it would be agin' my nature not to want to see Ernie planted! You understand that, Derby Man?"

"Yes. A year ago, back East, I thought there was no justification for hunting men this way. I'd have said a man who made his own laws was a barbarian."

"And now?"

"Now I know I was naive. We both have sworn to finish this, even if it means dying ourselves."

Everett nodded. "I just needed to know; sorry."

"Forget it," Darby said, reaching for a pouch of rough-cut tobacco. Absently, he dug out some paper and expertly rolled a cigarette. He reached down and picked up the end of a burning twig and lit his smoke. When he inhaled, he thought for the hundredth time about how he wished he hadn't run out of cigars. But in the crisp morning air, and over a last cup of coffee, the cigarette tasted good.

The two men stood staring out at the falling snow. Darby glanced sideways and knew that Everett was thinking and remembering Annie. The look was something he had grown to read well. When he watched the face, he could see it ripple with emotions as memory after memory passed through the man's mind. But it always ended the same way. The pain would streak out of the eyes and run down through the crosshatch of wrinkles, and finally it would conquer the whole face. Then it was bad; Darby would look away only to return his gaze several minutes later when the pain had given way to hard, taut hatred.

The cigarette was almost gone. Gently he pulled at Everett's coatsleeve. "It's time to ride. The light's good enough." He watched the man's face soften grudgingly. "Don't worry, we'll find him."

Darby stepped into the saddle and pulled the old rifleman up behind him. His eyes swept over the shelter he'd built and the dugout he'd carved for Everett that first stormy night. High above, the black, jagged top of a tree splayed out in frazzled contrast to the falling snow. It had been a good camp.

He reined the black out of the cottonwoods and they started toward Nevada. The soft, rhythmic shuffling of the gelding's hooves through the light snow rocked each man deep into his own private thoughts. Not surprisingly, both were remembering the Ratons. They passed the day lost in falling snow and images of things that had been and were to come. They were quiet, filled with a purpose that only a bullet would fulfill.

It was almost dark when Darby unsaddled the black and rolled in for the night. He faced south and lay staring, wondering how far. Just before he fell asleep, he decided it didn't matter. They were forty miles closer to the Ratons than they'd been the night before, and that was really all that mattered now.

"Jeezus! he's gonna prod 'em up and send 'em to do it tonight," Ernie swore, looking first at Abe Shipler, then at his identically outfitted brother. "What are we going to do?"

"Sit down!" the saloonman ordered. "We'll stop him, just sit down and let me think."

But Ernie wasn't through. "Sit down, hell! Ory Riley is forming a vigilante committee bent on lynching all of us, and you tell me to sit down?" he stormed in a voice that carried an open thread of contempt and disbelief.

From under his perfectly tailored black jacket, Abe Shipler casually produced a derringer. "Another word and you're dead!"

Ernie's feet went to rock. He looked at Junior and his mouth silently pleaded for help. But J. R. Raton was staring at the floor, not saying a word.

"Get out of here, Ernie. Me and him got some figuring to do."

"J.R., what's the matter with you, ain't you even . . ."

The derringer thumbed back and Abe Shipler extended it. Ernie suddenly broke and ran for the door.

"He's got a big mouth, that brother of yours."

"You were pretty rough on him, scaring him into thinking you'd kill him like that."

"I meant what I said."

Junior Raton ripped his eyes up from the carpet. "I couldn't let you do that, you know."

Abe sneered, "I couldn't let you try and stop me, boy."

The blood came pounding up somewhere behind his eyes, and Junior Raton stared at the man who he'd tried to imitate for the past two months. "Don't ever push me, Abe–or Ernie either, unless I say so. He answers to me."

"And you answer to me, J.R. Don't forget," he said with his voice rising. "I pay you, and him. Got it? I pay you, which means I own you."

I ought to kill him, Junior thought. Once he puts that gun back, I could, too. I could kill the mighty Abe Shipler! He found the idea amusing and he saw himself standing over Abe's grave. He'd take over and he could see himself as the only tailored, duded-up man in Mardis. The idea was very appealing. All it would take was a bullet.

"What the hell are you smiling at?" Abe asked suspiciously, feeling a cold uneasiness fingering at his chest.

"Nothing, nothing except how I'd like to get Ory Riley in front of my gun," he said mildly.

The response was so automatic that it caught Abe off balance. He stammered then blurted, "You could, you know. You could ambush him and I'd pay you enough to buy your own saloon. Nothing as big as the High Stakes, of course," he quickly added, "but I could set you up and, between us, we could squeeze every ounce of gold out of this town. I mean it, J.R., we could!"

"How much would you pay me to shut Riley up before tonight's meeting?"

"Plenty. I'd make it worth your while. It shouldn't be too

risky but I'd be willin' to go, oh . . . five thousand dollars, cash." He emphasized the *cash,* and waited for the shock of it to hit.

Junior Raton smiled icily, entirely unimpressed. "That's not nearly enough. If Ory talks, he'll stir those miners into hanging you. Abe, they'll flatten this place and you'll be dancing on air before tomorrow's sunrise."

"If you had gunned him like I told you that first day," Abe blazed, "none of this . . ."

"How the hell could I?" Junior snarled back. "He never comes to town and there's always a small army of his friends around him. Neither me nor any of the other boys have been able to get him in rifle range since the night I hit town."

Abe shoved the derringer angrily back into his coat. "I know, I know, damn it!" He began pacing back and forth across the plush gold carpet of his office. "Look, J.R., I'll give you ten thousand cash. I don't give a damn how you do it. Just kill Ory Riley before he talks to those miners!"

"Have you got that kind of money?"

Abe Shipler smiled. "I can get it, J.R."

"Good, then do, because I'll want the cash tonight on my way out of here."

A rebirth of suspicion flared across Abe Shipler's stony countenance. "Sorry to hear you'll be leavin'," he said, eying the younger man critically. "We might have made a hell of a team."

"And we might not," Junior added noncommittally.

"Could be you're right; we're too much alike."

"Just have the money, Abe—all of it!" Junior said, backing out of the door and moving across the balcony. When he descended the stairs he was smiling—he was going to use his gun.

On the trail of the men they followed, Darby Buckingham and Everett Randall passed around Copper Mountain and came to the head of Seventy-six Mile Canyon. The sun was touching the rim of the west wall and it was eight weeks to the day since the Ratons had gazed upon the same sight. Like the men they hunted, the view of the canyon and distant Mardis caught and held them.

A hard, biting wind, heavy with the promise of flat-blown snow, rushed by them. Down the canyon, it plucked and coaxed the dust from under the steps of both man and animal. Once it grabbed its catch, the wind blew its roiling, gritty vengeance down upon the town. Along the entire length of slicing Seventy-six Mile Canyon, Darby could see whipping billows of canvas struggling to overthrow the rocks that weighted their corners. Occasionally one broke free and sailed upward to flatten itself triumphantly against the high, rugged sides.

Though the air whistled, he could hear the ringing of picks that raced one against another until the whole sound of it seemed to erupt and be thrown from the walls themselves.

"Listen," Darby yelled into the blast. "They seem to be speaking. Listen!"

They listened and both men heard it and the longer they sat, caught up with the sound of it, the more clearly did the walls seem to speak of gold. Like countless men before them, their imaginations were swept away to run with the Nevada desert winds and listen to the humming of rocks that promised fortunes. Others believed–they should too.

Darby could see hundreds of miners crawling all over the canyon, digging, scratching, tearing–and they were listening too, always listening. They raced against each other, afraid the next claim would yield before theirs. It was man against man, and man against the canyon. Darby knew, as sure as he sat surveying it all, that the miners could beat each other, but they'd never beat the canyon. In the end, the rocks would bury many of them, and the sky would watch the others flee.

Behind him, Everett Randall shifted uneasily. "Let's get down this canyon before it talks us into rushing out to buy or steal some poor devil's claim. Listen long enough, it would make a miner out of any man!"

Darby grinned through his beard and gave the horse rein. They started their descent, wondering if they'd find the Ratons.

There was a graveyard up against the far canyonside. Darby considered the fair possibility they'd end up in it. He hoped not. It was a cramped and ugly place. Once, and it couldn't have been long before, someone had cleared away the vegetation. But that hadn't lasted a summer and the sagebrush stole back. Sneaking, it had pressed under stones and sifted through wooden and wire fences. It had made a slow, steady assault. It had won. As Darby and Everett rode by, tumbleweeds seemed to stare with round confidence. They leered openly, challenging them from all but the freshest grave sites. An almost dead sun shone weakly through a hundred busted whiskey bottles that lay scattered over the cemetery–Darby urged the horse into a trot–the bottles were as shattered as the dreams of the men who lay beneath them.

"Look"–Everett pointed–"there's a group of men gathering up by that rock."

"And more coming," Darby hollered into a windblown silence. "They've stopped working."

Figures floated out of the mines and the holes like shadows; they appeared everywhere. They were blinking and dusty. Most held a pick or a shovel, and, like lemmings, they all began to migrate toward the high rock that Everett had spoken of. They approached it from whatever angle they had emerged.

"Hey," Everett hailed at a group of stony-faced men, "what's going on down there? You fellas having some sort of meeting?"

None of the men looked up, but as they passed, one hollered back, "We're fixin' to form a vigilante committee and hang a few tonight; better stay out of Mardis, strangers, lest we hang you, too!"

Darby urged the gelding forward. "We'd better attend this meeting. If the Ratons are in that town, they are probably on the hanging list."

Junior Raton reluctantly unbuckled his pearl-handled revolver and placed it on the bed beside Ernie. Wordlessly, he slipped out of his tailored black frock coat and began to unbutton the stiff white dress shirt.

Ernie watched with immense amusement. "Well, well," he said grandly, "let's see how pretty you're going to look as a hard-working miner." He heaved a bundle of old clothes at his brother and giggled as Junior put them on. But when Junior had finished cramming his rough shirt into his pants, Ernie's face showed a disappointment.

Junior strode over before the mirror. "I still look good, even dressed like this!" he said, turning from side to side in frank approval.

"Don't forget to put on those work boots," Ernie said, feeling cheated but still hoping.

Junior eyed the worn, scuffed boots with open distaste. He sat down in a chair and slowly pulled off his own high heels and placed them carefully beside him.

Then he began to lace on the round-toed clompers. He fumbled with the laces and cursed the boots, knowing and not caring that he was making the show even more enjoyable than his loutish brother had hoped.

"Stand up and put this hat on and let's take a look at the new J. R. Raton!" Ernie said.

Junior took the thing and placed it over his head. The hat was as dead as rabbitskin and hung lifelessly over his ears and crowded his eyebrows. If it had once had body and form, Junior couldn't begin to imagine. He looked into the mirror and almost felt sick.

"Ha!" Ernie laughed victoriously. "Just as I thought.

Change the clothes, take away the big gun, and you're no better'n any of us!"

Junior's eyes bored into the glass, trying to see the image of a gunfighter in himself. It was not there. Furious, he spun around. "Shut up! Shut up or so help me God I'll kill you when we get this over with!"

Ernie ignored the threat. In comparison to the risks they faced tonight, the remark seemed tame. "Junior, do you think we can pull it off? I ain't sure we can; I mean, someone is bound to recognize us in the camps."

"Would you recognize me in the dark? Dressed as I am now?" Junior asked, sneering. "After the way you just laughed?"

"No, but . . ."

"No, but nothing. They won't recognize either one of us. It'll be dark and crowded. Half of 'em will be drunk from all the whiskey that Abe's been handin' out today. By the time they stagger into that meeting, most of 'em won't even be able to recognize Ory Riley. When he gets up in front of 'em and starts blabbin' about vigilantes, I'll slip this gun out and kill him."

Ernie shook his head. "I just don't see how we're gonna get out of there alive. There'll be a mob!"

"That's where you come in, stupid. You shoot anyone around us holding a lantern. In the dark, our gunfire will be echoing around the canyon, men will be diving for the ground —it will be a riot. By the time those stinking idiots recover, we'll be long gone."

Ernie tried his best to grin. "It might work," he said half-heartedly.

Junior smiled because he needed Ernie; nobody else would go along. "Sure it will work. Then we pick up ten thousand easy dollars. By tomorrow night, we'll be a hundred miles deeper into Nevada, but poor Ory Riley will only be six feet into her . . . straight down!"

"It's a gamble," Ernie said, still feeling something had been left out of the explanation.

"The stakes are worth it! Hell-fire, we'll never get an easier chance at ten thousand dollars!"

Ernie looked hard at his brother. "It's going to be okay? I don't want to die up there tonight," he said quietly.

Junior started to speak, changed his mind, and put on the gun and holster. He had chosen it well—it was worn but in perfect working shape.

"Now!" he breathed, and the gun came up fast, so fast Ernie couldn't see that the draw was any slower than the way he had always flashed the pearl-handed Colt. "Now . . . now . . . now!" Junior spat, eyes burning as he drew and holstered, drew and holstered. His hand blurred up and down until, finally, Ernie said, "Okay, okay! I believe you."

"I thought you would. Do you still think clothes change a man?"

Ernie looked at his brother. He saw the burning eyes, the smiling, arrogant face, the nervously twitching fingers. "No, no, J.R. I was dead wrong like always."

"Of course you were. Now get changed. At least put on a different hat and work boots; it won't be necessary to switch your shirt or pants, they already fit the part," Junior said cuttingly. Then, stretching: "Wake me, Ernie, when it gets on toward dusk. And stay sober; you got some work to do!"

Chapter 20

"J.R., wake up, it's almost dark and the whole damn town's deserted!"

He came awake fast, for even in his sleep Junior had planned how they'd do it. He grabbed the shabby hat, shoved it down hard over his forehead, and started toward the door.

"Are we just gonna ride in there?" Ernie asked.

"No, we walk, like they'd do," Junior snapped impatiently, "Don't be stupid; we wouldn't get halfway up the canyon horseback!"

Snorting in disgust, Junior went down the back stairs and hit the street without a break in stride. Behind him, big Ernie puffed as much from a nagging fear as from exertion. "How we gonna get away without horses, J.R.? How we gonna do that?"

"We leave the same way, only we run down, dammit! Unless you got any better ideas."

"No, but . . ."

"Why don't you shut up and let me worry. Sure we run a risk, a damn big one too. But they won't be expecting anything like this and it'll be dark. Hell, man, it's ten thousand dollars we're gambling on–and we'll win!"

"Jeezus, J.R., I sure hope so! I don't want to die yet."

Junior Raton walked even faster. Most of the time his brother just made him sick.

Darby Buckingham and Everett Randall tied the gelding to a piece of brush and sat down to wait. A drunk miner staggered by, eyed them curiously, then said, "You two look sober to me. Here, have a nip. But not too much—or I'll cut your arms off!"

"No thanks," Everett answered, but Darby's mouth and gullet felt sandblasted, so he took the extended bottle and upended it.

The whiskey was bad, very bad. He knew that before he even swallowed; the stuff seemed to grab him by the tongue like a pair of ice tongs. "*AH-aah!*" he spat, spraying the miner's pants.

But the miner didn't seem to notice. "Real good, ain't it, stranger?" the fellow said, retrieving his bottle and taking a long pull. His throat bobbed under his bandana three times, and Darby shook his head in amazement. "Yes sir," the miner gasped, wiping a clean smear across his dirty face. "I reckon I'll go see if old Ory wants a belt before he gets up to palaver. We picked him as our leader; no one else stood up against Abe's gunman the way he did."

"Who's Abe?" Darby asked.

"Who's Abe? Is that what you said? Tarnation! don't you know nothin'? Abe's the man been cheatin' us out of our gold all this time. He owns most of this town. It's him and his gunmen are the ones we're gonna hang. Especially those two redheaded gunners he hired!"

Everett Randall's breath sucked in hard and he sprang forward like he'd been unloaded from a bronc. He snatched the miner by the shirt front. "Their names, man, what's their names?"

"Wha, what, whose names? Dammit, let go of my shirt. Ish the only one I got!"

"Take it easy, Ev," Darby said, reaching out and unlocking the wire-tight fingers.

"Whassa matter with your friend? He change his mind and

wanna drink now? Thas okay, fella, you can have one still."

"No," Darby said, "what's the name of those two redheaded gunmen you mentioned?"

"Mud, mister. They're as good as dead!"

"Please, it's important we know."

"Well"–the miner pondered–"I ain't sure. They're brothers, though. You can see that much by the meanness that runs through 'em. One's big; busted up a couple men the first time he hit town. But Ory sure showed him a thing or two, yes sir! I was right there when it happened."

"Their names, damn you!" Everett choked.

"Jeezus, mister! Sure you don't need a drink? What the hell ails you?"

Everett grabbed at the man but there was enough sense left to blow out a whiskey breath. "One's named Ernie; that's all I know!"

It stopped Everett like the wallop of a buffalo gun. "Let's go," he said quietly; "let's kill 'em before this mob does."

"Kill 'em? You mean kill the redheads?" When Darby nodded, the miner seemed to sober. "Stranger, they've shot down two good men on the first day here. Busted up a bunch of others. How many more of my friends they've waylaid in the alley, I don't know." The miner took a quick pull and went on, "Those two are gonna hang proper for what they've done. If you by damn interfere and try to shoot 'em first, I swear we'll use the both of you to stretch our ropes!"

"But we owe them, too!"

"Then you can help us string 'em up!" the man said. "Now I got to give Ory a drink before he speaks his piece. Step aside and let me pass!"

They did, and the miner swayed toward the gathering. The two newcomers stood speechless and watched him go.

Junior Raton tried to look tired and affect a shuffle, imitating a worn-out miner. The work boots seemed excessively heavy, and he let them drag. Up canyon, they could see the light slanting down the road they followed. Sometimes it passed through shadow, but always the dust-filled ruts led them upward.

Ernie's eyes never left the firelight and he stumbled constantly. He was scared. "There must be a thousand of 'em up there, J.R. How we gonna get close enough? Hell, the whole top of the canyon's lit up like it was high noon!"

Junior Raton stopped in his tracks and felt a flood of defeat pass through his stomach. Ernie was right; it wasn't going to be possible to get within handgun range. Even if they did, too many men had lanterns. They couldn't knock them all out. A pair of late-arriving miners puffed by. Eyes glued to their footing, they were almost trotting. "Better shake a leg or you'll be late."

"Sure, sure," Junior mumbled, reaching down as though to tie his boot.

Both shot back disgusted looks but passed on. They were in a hurry. "For God's sake, J.R., let's get out of here!" Ernie whispered.

"No! There's got to be a way!"

"There ain't, I tell ya!"

"Come on, let's run back to town. A gathering like this is gonna take time; we can still kill Ory Riley!"

Thirty minutes later, Junior shoved a Winchester into Ernie's hand. "Let's ride back. Anyone who plans on becoming a vigilante will be there by now. That means nobody will try to stop us on the road."

"I don't like it, J.R. What if someone sees our horses while we're working our way in for a good shot?"

Junior Raton swung the huge-bored rolling-block .50 toward Ernie. "Right now—are you with me or against me? One or the other, I don't much care."

Ernie opened his mouth to protest, then shut it fast. He knew the sound would come out cracked like a dropped egg. In silence, he mounted and spurred his horse forward.

Junior laughed. "I knew you'd stick. Just think of the ten thousand, brother. Don't worry. I'll get you outa this alive and in whiskey money."

But the big man said nothing. He simply rode up the canyon, his knuckles wrapped white around his rifle.

They were halfway up when they stopped. The distance could be plainly judged by the bright glow that shot skyward to dance upon the dark-light rocks above it. The red lifted clear over the canyon walls; Junior guessed it could be seen for miles.

"Far enough," he whispered. "Let's go in on foot from here." He moved forward, feeling clumsy and big-footed in the work boots. The sound of strident, angry voices was clear. Passing around a boulder, they peered over and saw the crowd. One man stood on a glittering, fire-fanned boulder and spoke down at them. "You all know this is the only thing left to do . . ."

Junior eased down behind a rock and, very carefully, placed the buffalo gun out before him. "Go over there," he whispered. "Hit anyone who spots us. Pour the bullets in to put the fear of death on 'em–then run!"

"I will, oh, you know I will!" Ernie gasped in a voice that sounded like he'd already started running.

Junior elevated the rifle until the sights began to cover the rock below the speaker, then he started to worm it onto the man's body.

". . . the miners are the backbone of this town and we've been spit on long enough. Too many of us have been shot . . ."

The sights passed up the miner's left leg very slowly. They squeezed over his belt and caterpillared over his stomach.

". . . that's why we're here tonight to elect Ory Riley . . ."

Junior Raton felt an alarm go off inside. He flinched, tried to let loose of the trigger, but it was too late. A blast swept up the canyon like a flash fire. Men went down under the sound of it. The speaker flew straight backwards and lit twenty feet from where he'd stood. Nobody had to tell Junior he was dead; nobody had to tell him he'd shot the wrong man.

"Fire! Fire!" Junior yelled, and off to the side, Ernie Raton began to lever the Winchester like it burned his hands.

Everett Randall swung with almost fifty years of experience pointing him toward where the sounds were originating. His ears picked them out of the rocks below and isolated them from the booming echoes that were bouncing in from all sides. He saw the flashing of Ernie's rifle and he raised his own to fire. But there were too many men around him. It was impossible to get a clean shot in the melee. Someone, running blindly for cover, barreled into him. Everett slammed to the ground, but managed to keep the Winchester. When he came shakily to his feet, he reeled into the darkness, heading for his horse. Wildly swinging flashes of lanterns alternately blocked and blazed his way. When he found the horse, he tore its reins from the sagebrush, vaulted into the saddle, and sank spurs. The gelding panicked. Walleyed, it wheeled and raced out of control through the crowd. Two men were knocked flying, but Everett didn't know it–he was sighting in on the flashes down canyon. Let it be Ernie, he prayed.

Ernie saw the black, sinister-looking outline of Everett Randall charging out of the crowd and racing toward him. Junior saw him too; he thumbed the hammer of the big rifle to full cock and rolled the breechblock back. Cursing the single shot, he dug out a spent cartridge and crammed a fresh one into the chamber. The breechblock flipped forward in place behind it and Junior's eye came down upon the rear sight. He squeezed and the second high-powered blast seared up the canyon road.

Everett saw the flash of the buffalo gun; in the same instant, he slammed back in the saddle. His whole lower body seemed to go numb. He pitched forward, grasping for the saddle horn, trying desperately to hang on. His Winchester dangled by just his trigger finger. The pain kept him conscious and he unlocked his left hand from the saddle and brought all his strength to bear on lifting the rifle. He did. He brought it up, just chest high, and began to fire into the flashes that were coming down to meet him.

Ernie Raton's eyes closed on the silhouette and lights exploded before him. He screamed inside, then heard his heart stop and knew he was dead.

The gelding braced to a stop against the canyon wall. It was far from the dancing lanterns and the light was poor. But Everett Randall leaned out of his saddle and looked down at the man he'd killed. A long ways off, he could hear the receding sounds of a horse being whipped toward Mardis. He didn't care–this was enough. Everett Randall toppled forward and died before he hit the ground.

Chapter 21

Darby Buckingham knelt beside the thin, still body of Everett Randall. Around him, he could hear the uneasy shuffling of the onlookers; their lanterns glared brightly over the two dead enemies. He glanced at Ernie Raton and felt nothing. But Everett had been something special. In death, the deep facial lines and the stamped hardness had vanished. Everett suddenly looked years younger. At last, he was at peace.

Ory Riley rocked back and forth as alternating waves of vengeance and frustration washed over him. He wished he could have known the old rifleman. Finally he spoke. "We owe him a lot. He drew off the fire and saved plenty of good men tonight. Your friend had more than his share of courage. This wasn't his fight."

Darby's gaze left the familiar face, and he turned to regard the young miner. "Mr. Everett Randall was brave. But you're wrong in one respect–this *was* his fight. That man murdered his wife."

Ory's face convulsed. Behind him, a sea of vicious swearing rolled out at the uncaring form of Ernie Raton–the miners had heard.

"Gus Freeman," Ory said, jerking a thumb over his shoulder, "Gus is dead. The first shot caught him square in the chest. I'm the one they were after. Gus took my bullet."

Darby searched the man's face. It was sad that someone so

young could reflect such anguish. "You couldn't help that," he tried.

"No, maybe not," came the grudging concession. "But I sure aim to see that we get justice. It'll start with Abe Shipler. Ernie worked for him, mostly for his muscle. One thing certain, he didn't have the nerve to come up here alone. His brother was the bushwhacker; J. R. Raton, they call him. He's nothing more than a fast gun. Stop him and the others fold. I promise you, stranger, one way or another, we'll kill J.R." The way he said it, there wasn't a man in the crowd who didn't believe J.R. was the same as dead.

Darby Buckingham rose to his feet. It was time to head for Mardis. As he passed out of the crowd, the miners heard an unmistakable, "Not if I get to him first, you won't."

Junior Raton flogged a hard-breathing horse into town. The streets were deserted, plunged in darkness. Mardis was waiting for all hell to break loose. He slammed the animal into a sliding stop before the High Stakes Saloon and came out of the saddle running. When he lit on the front steps, the steely cocking of a rifle iced him in midmotion.

"Who's there?" cried a voice that seemed dangerously close to unraveling. "One more step and you're a dead man!"

"Don't shoot, it's J.R."

He could hear a flurry of hurried whispers, then a moment's silence. Finally, "Come in with your hands up so we can see it's you."

Junior shot a look up the canyon; the lights had moved, they were closer. He stretched his hands toward the sky, but he didn't want to–he wanted his gun in his hand. It was going to be that kind of night. When he held his arms up, they felt heavy, like someone had wrapped them in chains. He stepped toward the door and risked a final glance north. When he passed inside, his face was a mask.

"Damnation! J.R., what happened up there? We heard the shots. Did you kill him? Did you get Ory Riley?"

J.R. looked at the so-called gunfighters Abe paid. The fear on their faces fed his confidence. Suddenly he laughed. "Relax, all of you. Come on over to the bar and I'll set up drinks to celebrate. Riley's dead; the vigilantes are running for their holes–we shot the guts out of 'em!"

He didn't have to say another word; it was what they wanted to hear. Junior could sense the feeling of relief wash across the saloon like a wave. "Goddamn, J.R., I knew you and Ernie could do it!"

"Abe upstairs?" Junior asked, trying to sound casual.

"Yep. He's been waiting for you and . . . Say, what happened to Ernie?"

Junior turned, halfway up the stairs. "I told him to wait outside town just in case one of them miners would be drunk enough to run the wrong direction."

A tall man with a long, knife-scarred face broke in. "I don't like it. His story smells like rotten fish! I think something went wrong up there."

Junior's eyes stabbed through the man. "Weaver," he said softly, "are you ready to die? Cause if you're calling me a liar, that's what's going to happen."

Even in the dim light of the big saloon, Weaver's face went white until the scar looked fresh. He tried to outstare Junior but broke before he began. "No offense, J.R. I guess we're all sorta spooky tonight. Maybe, maybe I spoke wrong."

"You sure as hell did," came the answer. Junior Raton started back up the stairs. He stopped outside Abe Shipler's door and walked over to the balcony. The gunmen below hadn't moved. They stood grounded, staring up at him. "You boys might as well relax and celebrate. Those miners are scared. Only thing held 'em together was Ory Riley, and I told you he's dead. Ain't that right, Weaver?"

Weaver forced a sick laugh. "That's right, boys. If J.R. said he got him, he got him. Come on, let's have a drink and celebrate. Let's toast the Ratons, by damn!" When Junior went through the door, they were already starting toward the bar.

A weak candle struggled. Its flame cast light feebly over the table upon which it stood and covered nothing else. "Abe? You in here?" he said, quickly closing the door and stepping sideways.

"I'm here, J.R.," came the voice. "Did you kill Ory Riley?"

"Hell, Abe," Junior breathed, "I can hardly see you. Why don't you light some lanterns?"

"I'm expecting trouble, J.R. Don't seem smart to have the place all lit up."

"No trouble, Abe. You must have heard what I told the boys out there. Me and Ernie pulled it off. Ory's dead."

Silence cut deep. J. R. Raton dropped his gun hand, flexed his fingers, and waited, trying desperately to locate the voice. "Look, Abe, where the hell is the money?" he demanded.

"You sound scared, J.R."

"Go to hell, Abe! Just pay up and let me get out of here."

"Sure, J.R., I'll pay . . ."

Junior found him, at least he hoped he had. His gun came up and he shot, diving for the floor. A flash answered and Junior rolled across the room, emptying his Colt. When he stopped, he knew Abe Shipler was dead.

There was a full minute's silence. With his heart drumming against his ribs, Junior reloaded, then snaked his way through the darkness to where the body lay crumpled.

"You crooked bastard!" he hissed.

Down below, a shout went up, then Junior heard the sounds of running boots hit the stairway. "You cheat!" he spat. He stood up and kicked what was left of Abe Shipler. He could hear a yelling and pounding stampede as men charged up the stairs. Then Junior went through the window. He lit on his feet, running across the top of the porch. A minute later, he jumped into an alley and collided with a rain barrel. Spilling over it, he clawed to his feet and ran into the night. When he hit the back street, he saw two horses tied in front of the train depot. Nobody can stop me, nobody, he laughed. As he swung into the saddle and spurred south, the sounds of the horse's hooves beat out his laughter. He wished he could see it when the vigilantes tore Mardis apart.

Darby Buckingham tied the body of Everett Randall across the saddle and grabbed the reins. When he turned down the canyon road, the crowd of men parted. Beside him, Ory Riley walked in silence. There was nothing left worth saying—it was time for retribution.

Strange, Ory thought; a few minutes before they would have stormed into Mardis with the whiskey and the killing. They would have gone in yelling and tearing apart everything and anyone that stood in their way. Now, it was different. The miners were quiet. The whiskey was forgotten and its fire had blazed into a smolder. Now there was just an awesome, purposeful silence, more powerful than anything he'd ever beheld. He glanced over at Darby Buckingham and had the feeling that the strange man wearing the derby belonged in the front of it all.

So it was that they walked into Mardis with almost no sound save the dry crunch of leather on dirt and rock. They filled the street from side to side and fifty deep. It looked like some vast medieval army marching soundlessly in the night. For a moment they seemed to hesitate before the High Stakes; then Darby stepped through the swinging doors. There was a shotgun in his hands and the cold, murderous icicle that ran the length of his body numbed any compassion he'd ever known. His eyes swung across the cavernous interior, and the rifle barrel went with them.

"Upstairs." Ory motioned with his Winchester and began to strike toward the landing.

The man named Weaver stepped out of the upstairs room. "Jeezus!" he yelled, going for his holster. He never had a chance. Darby Buckingham slammed a load that took off the top of the wood staircase and blew Weaver into two more gunmen who had been following him.

"Abe! You and your men throw out your guns and come on down!" Ory yelled.

"Abe's dead," came a high-pitched voice. "J. R. Raton shot him and took off through the window!"

Ory turned and looked at the miners, who stood grim-faced behind him. "Throw out your guns and come on down, or so help me, we'll come up shooting!"

They waited. The voices upstairs could be heard arguing. Someone yelled, "Shut up!" and there was a moment's silence. "What if we do as you say? What happens to us?"

"You'll get a fair trial," Ory said. "It's more than some of you deserve, but you'll get it. It's either that or we'll blow you to hell!"

Darby Buckingham reached into his pocket and brought out another shell. He broke the shotgun, dug out the empty and shoved the fresh one in. When he snapped it together, the shout came down. "All right, we're coming!" A rifle sailed out of the room, then others followed. "We're trustin' you to keep your word, Ory."

Darby didn't wait to see them coming out, he was bulling for the door. Mardis would see that the gunmen upstairs paid. But Junior Raton must pay too.

Chapter 22

The sun struggled out of sage, peeked between an eastern line of piñon pines, and cast an angry orangeness on the dispirited rider. Its glow exposed a tired, drawn face and glistened on the stubble of new whiskers. The face wasn't young, and it wasn't old. It had probably been handsome once; this morning, it just sagged lines of weariness.

Sunrise was not kind to Junior Raton. It forced him to squint and it revealed his dirty miner's work shirt and a faded pair of rough-spun trousers. The trousers were mud-caked and tattered; they petered out halfway down his shins. The bottoms of his white legs chafed against the fender leather of his saddle to where they entered the hated work boots. His toes ached from constant pressure; even so, the big round-toed brogans kept slipping out of the narrow stirrups to dangle uselessly.

Junior felt washed out and empty, sterile even, like the miserably barren land around him. He hated the clothes he wore, and he hated the way they made him feel–like a nothing.

Twenty yards ahead, a jackrabbit vaulted onto the trail. Instantly, Junior forgot his dejection; here was something he could enjoy. A thrill coursed through him as his gun streaked upward. He whispered, "Now!" into his gunfire and chortled happily as the jack turned to stone in midair. The rabbit hung suspended, then crashed into the dirt squealing. He shot it again and felt good when it skidded backward. But the animal was still twitching and, somehow, it became very important to

Junior that he make the thing stop moving. "Yahh!" he hollered and whipped his heels into the horse's ribs. They charged forward.

The rabbit felt the earth's vibration running toward it. It began to kick with the last stringy strength it possessed, and it could see the brush to die in safely. But it was too late. Just before Junior rode it down, he jerked his horse into a slide. Hooves cut furrows big enough for planting, but they stripped alongside the rabbit and it continued to strive for cover.

"Git! Git!" Junior rasped, trying to spin his mount around. The horse swung about and its forelegs braced in fear. It could smell blood and it wanted no part of this game. When Junior tried to force it over the dying jack, the horse's eyes rolled and it went crazy with fright. Junior forgot the rabbit–here was something even more to his liking–the jack would die anyway. Man and horse, twisting and hurting, fought. Somewhere underneath them, the rabbit was stomped into nothingness.

It was over in minutes. Wrapped in a swirling cloud of dust, the horse found it no longer had the strength to convulse, or to even lift its head. It stood beaten, and its bit-torn mouth dripped into a crimson dirt stain between its feet. But the horse didn't care–it was breathing so hard it could no longer smell the blood.

Junior let the horse stand. The rabbit was no more than a stain with a few half-buried hairs attached to it. He had won. When he felt the horse could travel, he kicked it into a staggering trot. The trail of dust that cupped upward in their wake continued to sift and settle over the rabbit for a long time.

Three miles back, Darby Buckingham had reined in at the sound of twin shots. He sat and quietly watched a place where dust clouded over the sage brush. He wondered what he'd find when he reached the spot where the dust began to razorback into the distance. But despite the worry, he suddenly felt better. Now he knew he was closer than he'd dared hope–Junior was just ahead. The shots had rolled to him almost as one–it was Junior Raton all right, using a gun like only he knew how.

Twenty minutes later, Darby's gelding froze in a spraddle-legged standstill. It snorted, reaffirmed its fears, and spun like a cat. Darby was left sitting in air and crashed into the dirt. The breath was blasted out of him and, when he dragged in a new one, his eyes were staring at what remained of the jackrabbit.

Solemnly, he prodded until he had partially unearthed the mat. "No chance, Junior; nothing has changed since Running Springs. No chance is exactly what I'm going to give you. Fitting that the last thing you rob of life should be a rabbit!"

Junior Raton bullied his horse out of a dry wash and stumbled over a pair of railroad tracks. Cutting through a hill, they crouched flat and straight across the high desert, running for only God knew where. But they always went to towns; they fed this country like the rivers, so Junior felt confident. He allowed himself a generous swallow of water from his hollow-sounding canteen, then prodded his horse down the roadbed.

It was almost dusk when he saw the buildings. Unconsciously, he brushed at his shirt and tried to coil his exposed lower legs.

It was a big town, bigger than Mardis and maybe it had bigger opportunities for a man of his caliber. When you were the fastest, and willing to prove it, there always were opportunities.

He slid off the high gravelly roadbed and pointed his horse toward the main street. The animal smelled hay as they passed the livery; but, hell, he was hungry and thirsty himself. A drink first, he needed it badly; afterward, some new clothes—he'd be a new man.

Darby Buckingham jogged over the fresh tracks, departed from the roadbed where they had, and reined for town. His gelding seemed to step through the earth, so heavily did its hooves drop. Small wonder, Darby thought, it hadn't had a decent feed since they'd left the spring camp in Wyoming.

A weathered sign tacked with horseshoe nails clung to a rotting post. Elko, Nevada, was as much as it said. Unlike Mardis, this was a cow town–prosperous, permanent. Darby guided his horse toward the livery; maybe Junior Raton would be there. He eased his foot from the stirrup and pulled out the shotgun. There was no sign of life outside. He should dismount, he knew, and sneak in; but he was too tired, so he just rode into the dark interior with the gun leveled.

Expecting a shot, he heard nothing. It was a good thing, too, he thought disgustedly. With his eyes accustomed to the sun, the sudden dimness blinded him as effectively as if someone had dropped a tarp over his head. "Anyone in here?" he finally called. Silence.

Dinnertime, he decided, and plopped down unsteadily. He made a quick pass along the row of stalls, peered out the back door at a corral that held four or five very curious mules, then returned to the black. Darby felt thick-fingered and clumsy as he tugged at a sweat-soaked cinch strap. He tossed a saddle that seemed to be cast of stone over a top rail and laid a dollar in its seat. He put the horse into a vacant stall and unbridled it –that was easier–the horse's head hung only belt high. It took him a while to find a pitchfork, but it was worth the effort. At the first forkful, the gelding began to inhale the dry grass hay.

Satisfied the horse was well provided for, Darby retrieved his shotgun and started for the street. Once outside, he considered where to begin. Directly across from him, a burst of laughter rolled out of a saloon, and Darby started for it. His eyes were riveted on the swinging doors. Did Junior know he was being followed? No, he couldn't. Darby had kept too far back to be seen. His boots crunched solidly. But, surely he'd expect some . . . Darby discontinued the thought; it didn't matter, there was no turning back now.

When his boot hit the boardwalk, Darby cocked both hammers and stepped into the saloon with the shotgun waist high.

Everything stopped at once. If he'd tossed in a bag of rattlesnakes, he couldn't have grabbed their attention more completely.

"Don't move!" he said. Then, very slowly, he notched his rifle down the line beside the bar as if he were counting. A half-dozen men sat like statues around a faro table; Darby counted them too.

"Sorry to have interrupted your fun, gentlemen," he said as he backed out and started down the walk.

"Who the hell was that?" came the reaction when he departed.

"Damned if I know, but he's sure enough primed for bear. Better hunt up the sheriff; that dude is huntin' big trouble."

Darby was edgy, he knew. He'd burst into four bars and, each time, a double-edged knife seemed to plunge into his stomach. He'd attracted a crowd that grew with every entrance. Only two saloons left and he was running out of time.

The Waterhole Bar looked like any of the others, only it was quieter. Eight, maybe ten, men drank quietly, shoulder to shoulder. It seemed darker than some of the other saloons; then Darby remembered the Waterhole had no front windows. He held the shotgun low and crowded it in close against the railing as his eyes tried to pick out the face.

"Bartender," he said quietly, "a whiskey." Maybe he'd been wrong. Maybe Junior had just ridden through town–or gotten a room somewhere. Maybe . . .

His eyes weren't ready for it, but his ears picked up the quick scraping of a boot as it came off the brass footrail. Darby twisted and saw a shadow jump backward toward the room's center. The man had moved quick, too quick. Darby Buckingham threw himself away from the bar and, just before he hit the floor, he fired. The barrels erupted almost in his face. Sweeping everything in their path, they went through the chest of Junior Raton as his Colt was lifting. He died catapulting over tables and falling through chairs, and when he landed, he was like the jackrabbit.

Darby forced himself up. His ears rang and gunpowder hung like seacoast fog. What if he'd killed the wrong man? There'd been no chance to be sure. He dropped the shotgun and charged headlong toward the body. Crashing to his knees, he hesitated for a moment, then ripped the man's hat off. A great feeling of relief washed through him. He grabbed Junior by the shirt. "No chance, Mr. Raton, no damn chance at all!" he said, choking, as he shook the corpse up and down in anger.

"He's crazy!" someone yelled. "Get the sheriff. Grab the son of a bitch before he kills somebody else!"

Darby was staring into the blank, expressionless face, remembering Zeb Cather, when an arm locked around his neck in a strangle hold. His derby crumpled and he felt a searing pain across the back of his head. A rage came over him and he slammed Junior down and reached for the arm wrapped around his neck as he felt himself being ripped upward. Junior Raton was dead, but still he couldn't shake a gnawing feeling of helpless futility–the man had died too quickly. He found the fingers that were tearing at his throat. His iron hand plucked them loose and bent them back. Someone screamed into his ear. Then he was spinning around and every man in the saloon came in swinging.

Darby Buckingham fought with a joy he'd never experienced. He heaved and men flew back, only to charge forward again and again. He swung and punched until his arms grew weary and, for every blow he landed, he gladly took their best. And in the end, he was grateful for the darkness that had to come.

Chapter 23

Sound stabbed him into awareness. A voice droned in the distance and it brought pain. He tried to locate its source, but a maze of lines swam crosshatched before him. "Get up," the voice insisted. Darby Buckingham blinked but the blinking wouldn't work; his eyelids stuck.

"You're going to trial now," Jake Pettigrew stated. "Stick out your arms so I can latch on these cuffs."

Darby poked out his arms, felt the clasp of iron grate against wrists, and was prodded out the door into bright sunlight.

A crowd stood waiting in the street. Darby managed to clear his vision. He stared at the faces; they were openly hostile, not a friendly expression in the lot.

What passed as a courtroom was small and crowded. They had to wait for what seemed like a long time. Finally, the back door hinged inward from the alley and a mousy, gray-faced man made a stumbling entrance.

"Caught me at dinnertime," he muttered, wiping gravy globs off a vest Darby imagined to be cut from a dishrag.

"The court will rise for the Honorable Judge Smedley," the sheriff droned.

Darby rose from his bench, though most of the crowd seemed reluctant to follow suit. Small wonder, he thought. Smedley was hardly a man who commanded respect. He looked a seedy sixty, probably was actually in his fifties. Darby searched the face for something of character or strength. But he gave up when the judge asked, "That the man who's gonna get hung?"

Sheriff Pettigrew frowned; why didn't the old devil at least try and pretend he was presiding over a court of law? It galled him the judge took his oath of justice so lightly. "This is the *accused* party," he corrected in a steely voice layered with contempt.

The judge's lips came up and pouched out as his tongue dug at food stuck between his teeth. "Seems to me 'accused' is an understatement. Hell, the whole room is full of men saw the murder. Looks like half of 'em walked out of a mine cave-in," he drily observed. "Doc's been gettin' rich since early this evenin'–I aim to see that his business returns to normal. Look-a-here, how many out there saw that stranger barge into one saloon after another until he caught up with the deceased in the Waterhole Bar only to blow the poor feller apart with a shotgun?"

Half a dozen hands rose.

The judge poked his finger into his mouth trying to dig out the obstinate strand of meat. "Yew're goon to howaang," he garbled into his hand. Then, aware that not everyone had heard and some hadn't even realized a verdict had been reached, he stood up and proclaimed, "For the murder of a poor working stranger who was only mindin' his own business, I sentence you to hang!"

From under coats and out of boot tops, a collection of whiskey bottles shot up into a salute and a cheer rose. Judge Smedley bowed deeply and held the pose until he momentarily remembered his bald spot, then puppeted erect and magically created his own bottle. "Saturday morning, he hangs!" he squealed pompously over the courtroom.

Darby was shoved out the door at that moment. He felt suffocated and disgusted. Two men who had been standing just outside laughed at his unguarded expression.

He exploded. His manacled wrists hooked a chain upward and under the chins of both. With a roar of frustration, he heaved his arms up to hang the two gawking spectators like a woman's wash. They dangled kicking until Darby lowered them. With each hand he grabbed an ear, and then knocked their skulls together. When their eyes crossed, he dropped his arms and the two men toppled like cut cordwood.

When Darby turned away, he looked into a set of gray, smiling eyes. "They had that coming," Sheriff Jake Pettigrew drawled. "Them two never was worth much, and the trial was a mockery. Damn shame. Wasn't always like that. Smedley used to be a pretty good judge. But, hell," he sighed, "that was a long time ago. Come on, before the courtroom starts to empty and their friends realize what happened."

"You're safer in here than outside," the sheriff said, locking the cell and going over to his desk to sit down atop it. Slowly, he drew out a sack of tobacco and thoughtfully rolled a cigarette. The smoke rose and drifted lazily into Darby's cell. It smelled good.

"Say, Sheriff, I'd like a smoke. But all my tobacco and paper is still at the livery."

"You can use mine."

"I appreciate that, Sheriff, but there's other things in my saddlebags I need."

"Look, mister, I ain't no errand boy . . ."

"Sheriff, please. If I'm to hang day after tomorrow, at least allow me my possessions. There are some papers I need," he said. "I'd like to write . . ."

"You got a woman?" the sheriff said, with sudden interest.

Darby hesitated only a moment as he recalled Dolly Beavers. "Yes, I have a woman."

The sheriff shook his head in resignation. "Well, I guess it ain't her fault," he grumbled, going out the door.

He came back with the saddlebags and, after searching them, he handed everything between the bars. "I'll see she gets the letter," he said tiredly, "but it's a damn shame."

Darby took the thick sheaf of papers and placed them neatly on his bunk. A title, he thought–I need a title. He tried to think of something catchy, something that would grab an eastern reader's attention and sell. But when he wrote it, the title came as simply *The Legend of Sheriff Zeb Cather.*

Darby sat and stared at the words for a long time. The title was simple, not at all original, but it was right. He'd never written one like it before, but then he'd never written such a story–Darby left the words as they lay. He turned the pages until he reached the last lines he'd written, then reread them. Day after tomorrow it ends, he thought–there wasn't much time left. His pen hesitated only a moment; then he began to write. The story was coming to an end.

Everett Randall, though weak and as thin as any man I'd ever seen, was ready to ride. His leg wasn't fully mended but I hoisted him into the saddle. It was snowing lightly when we left our camp and started toward Nevada on the trail of the Ratons.

Darby Buckingham slipped back into time. His memory returned fresh and strong and he wrote of the trail they'd followed all the way to Copper Mountain. He remembered how the sun had played with its crest. He could almost see the majestic panorama of Seventy-six Mile Canyon. It had swept out to dominate Mardis at the flickering height of its glory.

The night passed; Sheriff Jake Pettigrew woke, stretched, and rolled a smoke; but still the words flowed. Darby was into the book and it transported him into another time. The small, mean cell, the pain of his recent beating, they were all gone–even the thought of tomorrow's hanging.

Sheriff Pettigrew watched his prisoner, aware that the man was totally lost in his writing. No doubt about it, he thought;

he is different. He just didn't fit into any mold or pattern. Soft-spoken, well-educated, but very deadly. Wears a derby hat, yet riding boots and a trail hand's outfit. Courteous to the extreme –yet without a trace of weakness. Jake Pettigrew scratched his chin in puzzlement; the man was a paradox. He knew he should turn his thoughts to other matters, but his curiosity wouldn't allow it. "That must be one hell of a good-bye letter you're sendin' to your little woman," he ventured.

Darby looked up, momentarily surprised at his surroundings. He hid the disappointment that crushed down on him.

"It's a book," he said quietly, "my last and best. Sheriff, you appear to be a man of your word; promise me you'll send this to New York. I have money for postage and some extra for your trouble. Do I have your promise you will mail it?"

"A book! Hell, man, I thought you said you were writing your woman. I been sittin' over there all morning just trying to imagine what a lady who got a letter like that must look like. A book! I'm plainly disappointed with you."

Darby smiled. "Sorry, . . . but your word; will you send it?"

The sheriff grudgingly nodded.

"Besides, I do have a woman. I intend to write Mrs. Beavers momentarily. But first, I shall put the ending to this."

Darby finished with, "I killed Junior Raton and I'm glad; I only hope they do not bury us side by side."

"There, it's done!" he exclaimed, rising and gathering up the papers. "Please send it as soon as possible with this money and my gratitude, Sheriff."

"I'll see it gets mailed."

The sheriff sauntered over to his desk and set the papers down carefully. Rolling a smoke, he looked over at his prisoner. "Stranger, you're downright abnormal–never, in all my time as a lawman, have I seen the likes of you."

Darby, feeling no appropriate response, moved to the barred window of his cell and peered up at the cloudless, blue sky. It was beautiful. So beautiful he stared at it a long time until it tinged salmon-pink and ran gold. He shut his eyes and felt very tired; he would sleep.

Sheriff Jake Pettigrew sat at his desk staring at the broad back of his sleeping prisoner. It was too bad a man had to wait around, knowing he was going to die. Much better to blow out a fella's candle with a quick bullet. He'd seen what the wait could do to a person–sometimes they cried, some called for the preacher, but most just wanted to get it over. Yet this one, this one just wrote and then went to sleep. It beat anything he'd ever seen.

He looked absently down at the papers before him. Then he blinked and peered closer. He was staring at what he supposed was the title page. Sheriff Pettigrew glanced over at the cell and started to speak, but his prisoner was asleep. Feeling somewhat sheepish, he turned the first page and, for lack of something better to do, began to read.

"Open up, Sheriff; the sun's up and that killer has lived long enough!"

"Yeah, bring him out. The noose is ready," someone else yelled.

Jake Pettigrew shifted in his chair, then slowly rose. "Are you ready, mister?"

Darby nodded.

The sheriff turned and walked to the door. He was surprised at the size of the crowd that waited. Most of them wore expectant faces and he saw that a few were drunk from a long night on the town. It was to be a social event.

"Vultures!" the sheriff said disgustedly. "I'll go get him for you." When he turned back to the cell, the crowd came rushing in behind him, filling the small office. Slowly, Pettigrew dug for a key. He took longer than necessary and their impatience amused him. Finally, he unlocked the cell and let it swing open, then turned to face them. He wanted to say something, opened his mouth to speak but, seeing the eagerness in their faces, he kept quiet. No chance, he thought.

A man carrying a fat, evil noose started to brush by him. The end of the rope trailed, and, suddenly, the sheriff stomped down hard. The rope jerked the onrusher around and Jake Pettigrew grabbed him by the shirt front and slammed him viciously against the cell wall. "Damn you," he snarled, looking into the startled face. "I'll bring him out! Get the hell away from here with that thing!" He turned to Darby. "Let's go. Don't worry about those papers. I'll mail 'em like I promised."

Darby shoved out his hand to shake, but the force of bodies surged hard against him, knocking him off balance. They were too tightly packed to fall, and Darby felt himself being propelled toward the outer doorway. The sheriff was wearing a sick look of helplessness. He's no Zeb Cather, Darby thought, but he's a fair man.

Jake Pettigrew slumped in his chair and ran his hands over his eyes to block out the day. When he dropped his arms to his sides, he was staring at the prisoner's writing. It was one hell of a story, he thought.

They had rigged up a platform for the hanging. It had been easy enough. An old freight wagon with a broken axle had been roped and dragged out to sag under a stark, leafless cottonwood tree. Inside the wagon, they'd carefully placed two empty fifty-gallon water barrels a yard apart. A rope coiled around each barrel. Facing inward from opposite ends of the wagon sat two mounted riders. The ropes ended on their saddle horns. Stretched across the top of the barrels was a heavy plank.

"Everybody's going to get a hell of a view!" a man exclaimed enthusiastically as Darby was shoved by. "Last time, some folks complained they couldn't see good."

"Look at the size of him! Neck like his oughta hold out past the drop," another said, swallowing involuntarily. "How 'bout another drink?"

A dozen hands heaved Darby into waiting arms on the wagon.

"You want to climb up yourself and put the noose on? Or do we have to do it for you?"

Darby slung the hands off. "I'll go."

The board was wobbly and his hands shook slightly as he climbed up. The plank groaned and bent, just as the spectators bent expectantly forward.

"It'll hold; I told you it'd hold!"

Darby glared down at the crowd. There must have been forty guns pointed at him. He forced a glance at the noose that dangled next to his face. The hell with this, he thought! I'm going to dive into them. Better a quick bullet. He tensed, rolled forward onto the balls of his feet. Suddenly . . .

"Wait!" The voice spun them around, and Darby, off balance, fought to keep from falling. "Hear me out!" Sheriff Jake Pettigrew bellowed, climbing into the wagon. "I ain't going to try and stop this. He had a trial. I can't deny that." Someone started to grab for him. Pettigrew shucked out his gun and the hand froze. "But before this man swings, you're gonna listen to a story." Then, not waiting for anyone to object, he hopped up and sat on one of the water barrels with the Colt in one hand and a slab of papers in the other.

The sheriff of Elko, Nevada, had never been much of a reader. The words came haltingly, and those he didn't know were skipped. But the story was good. It caught the spectators on the first page and carried them away to a sod dugout in Texas–to a boy fighting off Comanches. It breathed life into the Texas Rangers as they'd been before many of the listeners were ever born. Later, more than a few men found it hard swallowing after Annie Randall died alone in her cabin. Once, when the sheriff thought his voice would fail, he pulled a whiskey bottle out of a man's hand and drank. His voice came back, raw but husky, and he pressed on. The crowd was quiet until, at the place where Zeb Cather was gunned down, men swore softly. It was sunset when Jake Pettigrew croaked out the last sentence: "I only hope they do not bury us side by side."

It was over. The sheriff stared with bloodshot eyes across the crowd. "It's up to you. I won't stop this if you've still a mind."

They stood spellbound. Finally, one of the horsemen untied the rope from his saddle horn. Across from him, the other rider winked and did the same. A moment later, they were carrying Darby Buckingham on their shoulders, heading for the nearest saloon.

The next morning, the sheriff and most of the town stood looking up at Darby astride the black gelding. "Sure you must leave so soon?"

Darby felt a trip-hammer thumping in his head. It felt wonderful. "No thank you, sheriff. I couldn't stand another night of your excellent hospitality." He leaned out of the saddle and clasped the man's hand in a grip that almost squashed it. "Thanks," he whispered. He looked over the crowd of smiling faces. "Thank you all."

"Mr. Buckingham," the sheriff said as Darby started to rein away.

"Yes?"

"One thing I forgot to tell you."

"And that is?"

"You didn't really finish that story. Telegraph office returned my message this morning. Zeb Cather is alive and recovering."

Darby Buckingham galloped out of town and his laughter carried him all the way to Running Springs, Wyoming.